# ZANA WEST'S DIARY

#CaliGirls, #FirstCar, #Honolululaw

KATHARINE M. NOHR

## Advance Reviews for *Zana West's Diary*

"In this quick read, we meet Zana West as a young girl through her diary discovered years later by another teen. The story is thoroughly engrossing, giving the reader a view of Zana's traumatic childhood, and insight into the events that made her who she is today. A must read for fans of the Zana West legal mysteries."

—Laurie Hanan, Author of the Louise Golden Mystery Series

"Touching juxtaposition between the lives of two girls who are linked across years by a diary. *Zana West's Diary* paints a stark picture of life in the foster care system, and follows you long after it's finished."

—Tatiana McArthur, Author of *The Girl Behind the Numbers*

"*Zana West's Diary* is a book every teen and their parents should read. Katharine Nohr has presented the lives of two teenage girls, one of privilege and one facing the despair and desperation of the foster care system. Both girls' fears and emotions are laid raw for the reader to contemplate. Life is not always what it seems, and Ms. Nohr presents it in a way that tugs at your heartstrings. A read that is hard to put down."

—Flo Parfitt, Author of the Daughters of Evolution Series

"This is a gripping story of how one girl's horrors can provide the strength to others to carry on and succeed, despite their own problems."

—Scott Willems, ESL Teacher, East High School

"*Zana West's Diary* weaves a tapestry of privilege and suffering, resilience and hope as seen through the eyes of two teenagers who come from very different realities. It's an intimate look into a world of abuse and neglect and a reminder that hope and gratitude can be found in even the least likely places."

—Callie Trautmiller, Award-winning Author of *Becoming American*

"*Zana West's Diary* is a good read, and will connect with young adults interested in reading this genre, especially those who use social media as their main form of communication. A heart-warming story!"

—Stacie McGavock, Foreign Language and Bilingual Teacher, Crivitz High School

# ZANA WEST'S DIARY

#CaliGirls, #FirstCar, #Honolululaw

KATHARINE M. NOHR

Green Bay, WI 54311

Publisher/Executive Editor: Brittiany Koren
Copy editor: A.L. Mundt
Cover Art Designer: Ed Vincent/ENC Graphics
Interior Layout Designer: Katy Brunette
Ebook Interior Layout Designer: Maria Connor
Category: Young Adult Fiction

Description: A young girl becomes homeless after her mother dies and her father becomes a drug addict, yet still she dreams of becoming a successful lawyer.

Hardcover ISBN: 978-1-951375-20-1
Paperback ISBN: 978-1-951375-21-8
Ebook ISBN: 978-1-951375-22-5
LOC Catalogue Data: Applied for.

First Edition published by Written Dreams Publishing in July, 2021.

Green Bay, WI 54311

**The Tri-Angles Series**

**by Katharine M. Nohr**

---

***Land Sharks***

***Freewheel***

***VO2 Max***

# Dedication

*In memory of my loving Aunt Lois Wilson, who served so many in our family, her church, and community. She is sorely missed, but we rejoice in her joining her triplet sisters, my mom, Sharon, and Diane, and their parents, Devere and Merle Christensen with our Heavenly Father.*

*In special memory of my dear friend, Donna Good, who read all my books well before they were edited and published, and was always my biggest cheerleader. Donna loved animals, books, and was a gentle, sweet person, who will always have a place in my heart.*

# #Prologue

@ZLaw

My childhood was a nightmare. Now that I'm a successful adult, I'll put it out there. I was a foster kid. I was raped. And, sometimes I was homeless. I wish I'd grown up with 2 parents. But, that didn't happen. I had to make do with little and turn it into the life of my dreams.

# Chapter One

*@ZLaw*

The last few miles of a marathon can be agony. For me, my life marathon was a sufferfest from the beginning and only got worse with each mile.

*March 2000, Ventura, California*

Story Sanchez squinted through her sunglasses at the old blue car decorated with a gigantic white bow in the driveway.

"Happy Birthday!" Mom and Dad chanted in unison, and then her sisters echoed the sentiment.

Story hugged them each in turn and said, "Thank you." She'd asked for an off-the-showroom-floor 2000 Honda Civic for her sixteenth birthday, but in the Sanchez family tradition, was gifted with an ancient 1987 Buick Riviera. How could they give her something better than the old red truck her older brother Anthony had gotten on his sixteenth?

Story managed a real smile when she examined the car closely. It had a fresh coat of paint and the interior looked thoroughly detailed. The California license plate was personalized with "STORY 1," which made her laugh. She'd been named Stephanie Jill Sanchez at birth, but her parents had nicknamed her Story when she'd begged them to read to her as soon as she could talk. She loved stories of any kind. The name had stuck, and few of her friends even knew her given name.

"Hank restored it." Dad handed her the keys. "What do you think?"

"I like it." Story smiled. "Can I drive it?"

"Pass your test today and you can drive it all you want," Mom said, and then added, "within the rules, of course."

Story sighed. Her parents had rules for everything. Anthony affectionately called them "helicopter parents," because of their smothering involvement in their lives. That's why, as soon as he'd turned eighteen, he'd moved out and chosen a Florida university, even though he had better offers close by.

After a breakfast of homemade pancakes, maple syrup, crisp bacon, and fresh squeezed orange juice—all her favorites—Story and Dad headed to the Department of Motor Vehicles in his car. She'd been practicing in his BMW and didn't want to switch cars for the test. She felt fairly confident that she would pass the driving part. The butterflies in her stomach were caused by her anxiety over the written portion. She had never been a good test-taker.

When they returned home, Mom and her sisters—Kimberly and Betsy—greeted them at the door.

"Did you pass?" they asked at the same time, before she'd even got a chance to step in through the door.

Story frowned, hoping to fool them, but then cracked a smile. She jumped up and down in excitement. It was the best birthday present ever.

"Now, can I go for a drive?" She directed her question at her dad, because her mother would more than likely want her help with dinner or to assist ten-year-old Betsy with her homework.

"Sure." Dad nodded. "Don't go far and be back in an hour. You're not allowed to let other kids ride in the car."

Story didn't wait to hear the rest of his admonitions. She raced out the door to her very own car. She started the engine and carefully backed out of the driveway with her family watching her from the picture window of their spacious home.

She drove around the neighborhood, waving at a few kids from school. She was tempted to stop by Erica's and Whitney's houses, but there would be time for that later. Instead, she drove to the beach, found a parking space, and sat in the front seat, staring at the ocean and a handful of surfers waiting for the next wave. This was the first time in forever she'd been alone. She breathed in deeply, feeling her shoulders relax. She totally got why Anthony had moved far away to escape smothering suburbia and their *Leave It to Beaver* upbringing.

After a few minutes of relaxing, Story examined the car closely. The glove compartment was empty save for a manual, registration, and an insurance card. She got out and opened the rear door to examine the backseat. There was a small hole in the upholstery that she hadn't noticed before. She used the button in the front to open the trunk to calculate how much stuff it might hold—*if* she was able to convince her parents to let her take a road trip.

She ran her hand over the freshly vacuumed carpet in the trunk until she felt a bump. Was there something under it? *It's probably a tire iron or tools.*

She lifted it up, and underneath the carpet were three journals. She opened one, and on the front page it said, "Property of Zana West" in neat handwriting.

Before Story went to bed that night, she began reading the earliest entries in Zana West's Diary.

*March 6, 1992*

They won't let me go to school—again! We have to drive to Orange County for a stupid marathon. Mom would've let me stay with Ashley, but Dad said we have to go as a family. It wouldn't be all that bad, but there's a race every weekend and Miss Morris wants to have a meeting to talk about my attendance. I'm doing extra credit and she says I'm still the best student in Language Arts and Social Studies, but there's rules about attendance. She said something about the school's funding.

I slammed the door to my room. I hear them talking in the living room about me. It's hard to hear, but Mom said that I'm mad because I can't play with Ashley and Jessica on Saturday. Dad isn't saying much as usual. He's probably loading up the station wagon. He calls it an SUV, but it's a 1978 Chevy Mali-butt. It's not like Jessica's Dad's Ford Explorer. Mom doesn't want me to be mad. She said we can bring my bike and if there's a kids triathlon, I can do it if the fee isn't too high. I'd rather go to Disneyland, but it's too expensive. I hope we can stay in a motel. Mom says that's wishful thinking.

Maybe we'll camp in our tent. There's more room than sleeping in the car. I always get stuck sleeping in the back with my bike. Dad gets the backseat and he snores. Mom's knocking on the door. I'm ignoring her.

*March 7, 1992*

I couldn't sleep last night. I could smell Dad's feet hanging over the backseat, so I draped a t-shirt over them. It didn't help. I forgot to bring a pillow and had to use my backpack. Now, I have a headache.

I finally fell asleep around 4 A.M., but a few hours later roosters woke me up. Dad parked the station wagon near some farmhouses and a man wearing overalls knocked on the door and told us to move along.

We found a place serving breakfast for $1.99 and split two plates. Well, Dad ate a whole plate and some of the second plate. I had toast with grape jelly and some eggs. I'm still mad about having to come to Orange County so I'm not talking to them, except when necessary like asking to use a bathroom.

They don't have much money, so they dropped me off at the library. They're checking out the marathon course. Dad said he's sick of my sullen attitude. Mom smiled and said I'd be in a better mood after spending time alone.

If I were talking to them, I would've said that if they didn't want me hanging around, why didn't they let me stay at Ashley's house? Parents can be so stupid. A lady is reading aloud from a Dr. Seuss book to some kids a few years younger than me. When I'm done writing in my diary, I'll find *To Kill a Mockingbird*. My teacher said I'm like 4 grades ahead in my reading and writing skills.

Mom would like me to skip a few grades, and since I'm the tallest in my class, Miss Morris agrees. Dad says I'm too immature and he doesn't want me to get mixed up with boys. I'm not sure what he's talking about. Maybe their feet smell, too.

*March 7, 1992—5:40 P.M.*

I'm still at the library. My stomach's growling and my head hurts. The librarian has been staring at me and frowning for hours. She finally asked if she could help me. I assumed she was asking about books, and so I told her I couldn't find *To Kill a Mockingbird* anywhere. She finally cracked a smile and said my classmates had checked out all the copies. Apparently, it's on some class reading list and she assumed that's why I was asking. I didn't set her straight.

It's almost 6:00. I keep looking out the window for the station wagon. The library will be closing soon. I guess I can sit on the front steps and wait for my parents. I don't have any money and haven't eaten since breakfast. I'm bored.

*March 7, 1992—5:53 P.M.*

Some of the lights have been turned off. I guess they want me to leave. There's no one else here except that librarian with the long gray hair and her jangly keys. If she's not staring at me, she's staring at the clock. Maybe she has a date or has to get home to feed her cat. She's coming over here.

*March 7, 1992—6:12 P.M.*

I found a bench to sit on, but I'm not alone. This weird guy who talks to himself is sitting here, too. Sometimes he stands up and yells swear words. There's no other place to sit and if I focus on writing, hopefully he won't bother me. I wish I could've checked out the book I was reading, but I live too far away to return it and I don't think my library card for Ventura will work here.

I hope they didn't get in an accident. What if they were sick of me not talking to them and they abandoned me here? All I can think about is food. I drank as much water as I could from the drinking fountain to fill up my stomach, but now I have to go to the bathroom again. There's a black van pulling into the parking lot.

*March 7, 1992—8:45 P.M.*

I'm writing this by flashlight under covers in an actual bed. Everyone else in the house is asleep, because they have to get up at 3:30 in the morning to run the marathon. I have to go with them, because I can't stay here in Mr. and Mrs. Reed's house alone. They're also triathletes and when the station wagon broke down, Mr. Reed picked Mom and Dad up in his van and then stopped by the library to pick me up.

I said I was hungry, and Mr. Reed gave me a Kind bar from his gym bag. All they do is talk about triathlons and the marathon, so they barely noticed me at all. Mom sat next to me in the backseat. When we'd almost got to the Reeds' house, she put her arm around me, kissed me on the cheek, and said she loved me. I smiled at her for the first time in weeks.

Everyone says I look just like her. She's tall with straight black hair and green eyes. She's much prettier than I am. I'm not talking to her just yet, but maybe I will tomorrow.

This house is huge compared to our apartment. I'm sleeping in the same room as their five-year-old daughter, Zoe. They were laughing at dinner, saying how cute it was that their girls are named Zana and Zoe. The zany Zs, they called us.

I don't think Zoe is zany at all. She has curly blond hair and stares at me with big blue eyes, then giggles and runs away. I hope we can leave tomorrow after the race. I heard Dad say that the station wagon needs a new battery. I wonder what a battery costs. If we don't have money for Disneyland, a kid's triathlon entry fee, or to buy food, we might be stuck here. Dad always says I worry too much. He never seems to worry about anything, so I worry for both of us.

*March 8, 1992—7:15 A.M.*

I walked with Mom and Dad to the marathon start line. Mr. and Mrs. Reed dropped us off before taking Zoe to her babysitter's house close by. Mrs. Reed's in Mom's age group and they joke about kicking each other's butts. Dad is the oldest, but they say he's the fastest, so he started near the front. They told me to stay near the finish line and Dad should be done in two hours and forty-five minutes.

I'm sitting on a park bench. I wish I could lie on the bench and go to sleep. It's like this every weekend. We're always going to triathlons or running races and I'm stuck getting up in the middle of the night and hanging around at the finish line. They can't afford a babysitter and since I'm super tall and mature for my age, they said I could take care of myself. Some people think I'm twelve years old, but I'm only eight. They don't get that I'm scared to be by myself. I started crying when I said goodbye to Mom this morning. I hugged her tightly and whispered, "I love you."

She looked happier than I've ever seen her. She said, "I love you, Z-bear," like she always does. She skipped to the start line. I guess I'm talking to her now.

*December 26, 1992—9:48 P.M.*

Dad gave me this diary for Christmas. He said it would help me to write about my feelings. I don't think he knew that I already have a diary—an old school notebook. At least this one has lined pages and a blue cover with a butterfly design. I'm not sure why he thinks I'm the one who needs it. He's the one who needs help. He started smoking pot about a week after Mom died and now, that's all he does. We had to move into a super small apartment, because he lost his job at the bike shop.

At first, he tried to hide the joints and bong from me, but now he doesn't seem to care. He sold all of our bikes a few weeks ago to get money for drugs. He said the money was for rent—another lie. Does he think I can't smell? This apartment is so small—he sleeps in the living room and I have the closet-sized bedroom.

I can hear him and his friends in the next room. Dad supplied the pot for their "party." There's no way I'm going to get any sleep tonight. They're talking loudly. It's smoky. I have to pee, but I don't want to go past them to get to the bathroom. At least, I don't have to get up early tomorrow for school.

I wish I had grandparents or aunts and uncles like the kids at school. I would live with them instead of my stoner dad. I can't even go to Ashley's house anymore, because we moved too far away. I have to go to a new school now, and the kids call me Giraffe or Stretch instead of Zana. I haven't made any friends yet, so all I do is study.

At recess, I help out the librarian by putting books away. After school, I walk to the free community pool and swim laps until open swim is over. Christmas vacation is torture. No school lunch. I sit in my room all day. Sometimes I cry. I miss Mom.

# Chapter Two

When Story woke the next morning, the first thing she saw was her car key on the nightstand next to her. She smiled at the thought of telling her best friends, Erica and Whitney, about her present. Story's parents had thrown her a Sweet Sixteen birthday party on Sunday with hot dogs, chips, cake, and ice cream poolside in their backyard. A dozen girls and boys she'd known most of her life were invited to celebrate. They'd horsed around in the pool for hours while their parents watched and chatted amongst themselves. Her real birthday was yesterday—the day she'd reserved for her driver's test.

She wished she could pick her friends up in her car for a drive to the beach, but that was against "the rules." *Sigh.*

She lay in bed for a few moments and contemplated going back to sleep. It was summer vacation. Her parents wanted her to enjoy being a kid, so there were little demands on her. No part-time job, no classes, no camp—only play and relaxation for two whole months.

That girl's diary was open next to her on the bed. Story looked at the inside cover again. Her name was Zana West. What a strange name.

"Story," her mother said as she walked into her room without knocking. "I made pancakes with the leftover batter."

"Do you mind knocking?" Story had only had her own room for a few months after begging her parents to move her belongings into Anthony's after he'd announced he'd be staying in Florida to work over the summer. She'd shared a room with fourteen-year-old Kimberly for years. Her parents had reluctantly agreed when Story commented that they'd probably get along better if they didn't share a room. It wasn't like they fought all the time. Only when Kimberly took her hairbrush, didn't clean up the room, or cracked her knuckles. That was so annoying.

Her mother didn't respond to her comment but went back downstairs. Story could smell the aroma of pancakes and bacon, and her mouth began to water. She crawled out of bed with the diary in hand. It wasn't as if it was her own diary, but she slipped it between her mattress and the box spring out of habit.

As soon as she reached the kitchen, she gave her mother a tight hug and said, "I love you, Mom."

"Wow! I love you, too, sweetie," her mom said with wide eyes.

*January 7, 1993—7:37 P.M.*

I made a friend today. At lunch, Kelsey Pang asked if she could trade her apple for my orange. I like oranges better, but swapped it anyway so she might sit with me. She did, and we made fun of our math teacher who starts every class with, "We're going to learn loads today." He's English. Kelsey can imitate his accent perfectly, even though she's Chinese. I asked her if she's from China and she laughed. She said she's from Pasadena. Her family moved here last month, and she hasn't made many friends, either. The best news is that while we were talking, Kelsey's friend, Tania Wu, joined us. It turns out that she also swims at the community pool and has done a kid's triathlon. You should have seen her face when I told her I've raced in 8 triathlons and have won my age group a few times.

Kelsey looked confused, so I explained that a triathlon is a swim, bike, and running race, and the kid's version is very short distances of each sport. She thinks it sounds fun, but she doesn't know how to swim. I told her I'd teach her.

The bell rang and we had to go to class. That afternoon, I swam next to Tania at the pool. I wanted to tell Dad about my new friends, but he was passed out on the mattress in the living room when I got home. I made a cup of noodles for dinner again and ate it in my room. Now I smell pot smoke, so he must be awake.

*January 28, 1993—8:30 P.M.*

Weird day. Dad was waiting for me at home with a bag of filet of fish sandwiches and fries from McDonalds. We ate dinner together while sitting on his mattress, since we don't have any other furniture in the living room. He acted like everything was normal—as if we did this every day.

He said, "Z-bear, let me tell you the story of how you got your name."

I've heard it a million times, but he went on with it anyway, and told me that they combined Mom's name, Dana, with the Z in his name, Zachary. I nodded and smiled.

He wasn't high on drugs. It felt strange to have Dad back to his normal self. He even asked about school.

I told him about the A+ I got for the story I wrote about the trip we took to Kona when he competed in the Ironman Triathlon. We were supposed to write about the most exciting thing that happened in the past year, but I didn't want to write about Mom's heart attack at the finish of the marathon. The Kona trip was last year, but my teacher wouldn't know.

Dad beamed when he saw my grade. After he read the paper, he had tears in his eyes. I know he misses Mom, too.

*March 8, 1993—11:22 P.M.*

I can't sleep. Last year on this day, Mom died in the hospital. I shook Dad awake this morning and yelled at him (and cried) and begged him to write a note excusing me from school this afternoon for a dentist appointment. After pulling teeth (ha ha!), he wrote the note and then passed out again. Whatever.

I wanted to go to the cemetery by myself anyway, so I took a bus after lunch. I don't have any money for flowers and picked a few roses from gardens I passed. I took a flower from about 5 arrangements at the cemetery. I looked around first to make sure no one saw me. It was empty.

It took a while for me to find her grave. Dana Kamilah

Gamal West was born on February 16, 1963 and died on March 8, 1993. She was thirty years old. I used to think she was really old. I wish she'd lived to be a grandma.

Every day, I hear her voice telling me what to do. "Zana, it's time to get up." "Don't forget your sweater." "You can watch TV *after* you do your homework." "Brush your teeth." If it weren't for her voice in my head, I'm not sure I could even get out of bed to go to school.

I try to remember what she told me about her childhood, but it's all so fuzzy. All I can remember is that her dad was from Egypt and her mom was from Ireland, and they'd moved to California because their parents didn't approve of their marriage. They died in a car crash before I was born, so I never met them.

I wonder if Mom knows that I went to see her today. I wonder if she knows that Dad started using drugs after she died, and he doesn't do triathlons anymore. I hope she knows I'm working hard at school and learned how to cut my own bangs, so I look just like her.

*May 20, 1993—8:49 P.M.*

Kelsey is going to summer camp and Tania is spending a month with her dad in Texas. When they asked me about what I'll be doing, I change the subject. Tania pressed me today and I told her I was hanging around home. I still haven't told them about Mom and I've never invited them over.

After school, I go to one of their houses almost every day and their moms give us after school snacks. At Kelsey's, we eat pizza bites or cookies and milk, and at Tania's, we usually eat apple slices and carrot sticks. If they came here, they'd get tap water in a mug with a broken handle.

I wish I were old enough to work or move out of here. Dad got a job working at a warehouse a few weeks ago. We bought cereal, milk, bread, peanut butter, and fish sticks when he got his paycheck. He must have been fired, because he stopped going. Now he sleeps on his mattress or smokes pot when he's here. He disappears for days at a time and leaves me with no food or money. At least during the school year, I can eat school lunch and the school has breakfast for needy kids like me. Snacks at my friends' houses are dinner.

I'm not sure what I'm going to do next week when school is out for summer. A few kids at school have paper routes, but I don't have a bike anymore. My plan is to spend as much time as I can at the library and the community swimming pool. All I have to do is figure out a way to get food.

*June 28, 1993—9:15 P.M.*

Mrs. Cabot, one of our neighbors, invited me to her apartment this afternoon. I was super hungry and had opened a trash bin to see if someone had thrown something good away. It was the first time I'd ever done this. I think she was looking out her window, because she came out and shook her head. She said I'm too skinny. She said I look like skin and bones and told me to come in for cookies she just baked.

I sat at her big wooden kitchen table and she made me a grilled cheese sandwich and tomato soup. I drank two full glasses of milk and downed four chocolate chip cookies. While I was eating, she asked me lots of questions about Dad. The school counselor had asked me some of the same questions last month, but I told her Dad took good care of me.

I didn't want to lie to Mrs. Cabot. She's very nice and has a lot of food in her fridge. After I told her about what Dad does during the day, she frowned and was silent for a long time while I finished the plate full of cookies.

As I was leaving, she gave me a few hard-boiled eggs and a banana in a brown paper bag for breakfast. I felt so choked up, I could hardly say anything. It's been ages since I've had breakfast.

Now that I've had some food, my headache has gone away and I'm able to read again. I should feel good enough to go to the library and swim tomorrow after I eat my eggs and banana, which are next to my bed for safe keeping.

Our power was turned off a few days ago and the fridge doesn't work. I have a flashlight I can use at night to go to the bathroom, but I don't want to wear out the batteries, so I only use it if necessary. I haven't seen Dad since last week.

***

Story unbuttoned the top button of her shorts after their dinner of roast beef, mashed potatoes, carrots, string beans, homemade rolls, and boysenberry pie with ice cream. Mom always cooked a big meal on Sundays and today was extra special, because Anthony had flown home for a week's long visit. Story didn't mind giving him his room and moving back in with Kimberly during his stay. She hadn't had a chance to redecorate yet. His Red Hot Chili Peppers and Foo Fighters posters were still on the wall. She planned to replace them with NSync and the Backstreet Boys the next time she got paid for a babysitting gig.

"You look well-fed," her brother said after dinner.

"Thanks a lot!" Story socked him in the arm. She tried not to act like his comment hurt her, but she knew she had gained weight now that she was driving everywhere instead of walking.

Over dinner, Anthony talked about his classes. He'd declared a business major, but was thinking about switching to psychology against Dad's advice. Story noticed how animated he was when he talked about his psychology classes. He had even gotten a job as an orderly at a mental health hospital.

"Well, if you go into medicine, you could be a psychiatrist," Dad suggested.

"I think I'd rather be a family therapist," Anthony said.

A round of raised eyebrows followed.

Anthony had never struck Story as someone who cared about anyone's feelings or problems. He had always been her self-centered big brother. Instead of engaging in conversation, he had often been sullen or unresponsive to all attempts to include him in family discussions.

"I know, I know." Anthony smiled widely. "University has changed me. I've been dating a girl who's helped me open up about my emotions."

This was the first time Story had heard her brother mention a girl or use the word emotions—all in one sentence. They all listened in rapt attention as Anthony described Brooke Fernandez, whom he'd met in his co-ed dorm. She even lived on his floor. Her family origin was also Argentinean—from Rio Gallegos, rather than Buenos Aires, where Story's paternal grandparents still lived.

"Are you sure you want to change majors, because of this girl? You've done well in your business classes," Dad said, then paused. "What will happen when this relationship ends?"

Anthony's face turned scarlet. "We're engaged, Dad."

Story jumped up and gave her brother a congratulatory hug. She had so many questions. *When were they getting married? Would the wedding be in Florida? Would she finally get to go to Epcot Center and Disney World?*

***

*June 30, 1993—6:53 P.M.*

When I got home from the library today, Dad was lying on his mattress, but there was a business card on the floor from Child Protective Services. I picked it up and asked him what it was. He groaned, then mumbled he promised to do better. I'm not sure what's going on with him. He looked super skinny, his eyes a yellowish color, and his hands were shaking.

Mrs. Cabot gave me a brown paper bag with a peanut butter and jelly sandwich, an orange, 3 cookies, a banana, and 2 hard-boiled eggs when I walked past her apartment. I put the banana and half of the sandwich and an egg on a plate for Dad and put it on his mattress, then I went to my room to eat the rest. Now that Dad's back, I'll eat everything else in the bag. If I save something for breakfast, he might find it in my room and eat it, too.

*July 4, 1993—3:30 P.M.*

It's going to be a long day. I'm stuck in my room while Dad is having a 4th of July party with his friends. I smell cigarette smoke. When I couldn't hold it anymore and had to walk past them to go to the bathroom, I saw a skinny lady inject a needle into her neck! I felt like I was going to throw up, so I turned my head away.

It's quiet now, because everyone is quiet. Some of them are sleeping on the floor or on the mattress. I got a drink of water from the sink, and since no one was paying any attention to me, I took the half-eaten bag of potato chips to my room.

I'm halfway through reading the stack of library books I checked out. I just finished the *Pelican Brief* by John Grisham. I like his books. Maybe I could be a lawyer someday.

The librarian didn't want me to check out these books, because she said they're too old for me. I can read them, but sometimes they're hard to understand. I read *She's Come Undone* by Wally Lamb last week. It was really good. It's about a girl, Dolores, who gets fat from eating lots of food. I don't think that could ever happen to me.

I hear people laughing outside. I wish I could go to a picnic and watch fireworks tonight. Mom and Dad used to take me to a park for the 4th of July after they raced in a triathlon or running race. We barbequed hot dogs and ate corn on the cob. I would like to shake Dad and tell him to get up so we can go to the park. But I know he won't be able to go. I heard him talking about using smack. I researched it in the library and learned he's talking about heroin.

*July 5, 1993—6:09 P.M.*

Dad was passed out when I left our apartment after 6 last night. I walked about 3 miles to the beach. There were families having picnics and kids were playing and swimming. I didn't think to bring my swimsuit or a beach towel. I found a piece of cardboard and sat on the sand. Some kids came over and started talking to me. Their family was on vacation from Fresno. When their mom called them to eat dinner, she offered me a plate of food. She gave me a hamburger in a bun with lettuce, tomato, and mustard, a dill pickle, potato chips, and corn on the cob and a can of cold root beer.

I sat with the family on their blanket while we ate. The older girl, Ellie, said I ate fast. I tried to slow down, but I was really hungry. I told them that my parents were at work and they were going to meet me in a few hours. The mom seemed worried about me being alone. I told her it's all right, I'm used to it.

I think they thought I was a few years older than I am, because I'm so tall. I pretended to be older, which I often do. I'm super polite and I use words I've learned in books I read and sometimes I try to act like the characters. At dusk, I thanked the family and left.

I was so scared when it got dark and the fireworks were making loud noises that sounded like guns. I ran as fast as I could. I don't think Dad noticed I left, because he was in the same position when I got home.

# Chapter Three

On 4th of July, Story helped her mom and Kimberly in the kitchen prepare potato salad, corn on the cob, a lettuce salad, and strawberry shortcake to be taken to the beach where they'd barbeque hot dogs and hamburgers. When everything was ready, she begged her parents to let her drive in her own car. They agreed, and suggested Anthony ride with her.

"Are you going to get married in Florida?" Story asked as she pulled out of the driveway. "I've wanted to go to Epcot Center forever."

"Whoa," Anthony said, "we haven't even set a date yet. We might wait until we've graduated."

"Does Mom know this? I think she's already researching caterers for your reception."

Anthony sighed. "Can you keep a secret?"

Story nodded. He didn't have to ask. They'd always been confidants—ever since he broke their mom's favorite coffee cup and she hadn't spilled the beans, even when all the kids were grounded for the day.

"Brooke and I are living together."

"In the dorm?" She turned her eyes temporarily away from the road to look at her brother. He was twisting a rubber band between his fingers.

"No, an apartment. We moved in at the end of the school year."

"She's not pregnant, is she?"

Anthony laughed. "No. We're sick of the dorms. With Brooke's waitressing money and my paycheck, we can afford the rent."

"Are you sure you don't want to tell everyone?" Story asked. This was the biggest secret he'd ever asked her to keep.

He shook his head no. "I'll tell them eventually. For now, I want to relax on the beach, eat barbeque, and hang out."

They pulled up and parked next to their dad's SUV.

Story piled her paper plate high with food, listening to her family members tell stories about their favorite Fourth of Julys. This was the first such holiday in ages that they'd only ventured a few miles to the beach. For years, they'd celebrated on road trips. They'd traveled to the Grand Canyon, Palm Springs, the Oregon Coast, San Francisco, and they'd even driven all the way to Vancouver, British Columbia one year. Her parents insisted they be together as a family, enjoy delicious food, and light fireworks.

***

*July 13, 1993—8:15 P.M.*

The lady who stopped by to talk to Dad came back. She said they're going to put me in foster care. Dad told her that I'm staying at my aunt's house, but I was sitting in my bedroom and heard everything. She asked when I'd be back, and he said he didn't know. She demanded to know "my aunt's" address, but Dad wouldn't tell her anything. They yelled at each other and then she left.

I pulled my blanket over my head so when Dad came in, he couldn't see my face. He didn't sound like he was on drugs and promised he wouldn't let them take me away.

The electricity is still off and the only way for me to get food is from Mrs. Cabot. Yesterday, she said she hadn't gotten groceries so she could only give me a bowl of cereal and an apple. She looked sad. I think I'm going to foster care soon.

*July 15, 1993—10:34 P.M.*

Dad brought home a loaf of white bread and a jar of peanut butter and he made a sandwich for me. Before Mom died, I would've complained about there not being any jelly. I don't complain anymore. I ate it quickly, then rinsed my plate and put it in the cupboard.

Dad asked me if we still had Mom's sewing machine. I told him that he sold it. Later, I covered it with my dirty clothes in the closet.

*July 23, 1993—6:30 P.M.*

I have to focus on something good. School starts in 3 weeks. I get to see my friends and eat breakfast and lunch. I'll have something to do. I'm bored. I'm hungry. I have a cold.

I took an extra roll of toilet paper from the library bathroom. Kelsey's mom buys tissue in boxes. It's soft. I've filled up a trash bag with toilet paper already and my nose is bright red from blowing.

Dad found Mom's sewing machine. It's gone.

*July 30, 1993—4:42 P.M.*

I cleaned my room today. There was a power outage, and the library and the swimming pool closed early. Mom and I made most of our clothes using her sewing machine. I've grown another inch since she died, but I'm much skinnier so I still fit in my clothes. My pants are getting short on me and my dresses are now short the way I like them. I fit into most of Mom's clothes now, so I have some "new" clothes for school. Mom's shoes are a little small, but so are mine, so I'll have to wear the sandals, because they don't pinch my toes as much.

Someone is knocking at the door. Dad's not here.

***

Story stepped on a layer of clothes—both clean and dirty—strewn across the floor on her way to her unmade bed.

She pushed stuffed animals aside and lay down against a pile of teal, purple, and pink pillows. She reached for the TV remote and clicked through the channels before settling on *The King of Queens*. She'd seen the episode before, but watching it made her relax. It wasn't like there was much going on in her life that she needed relaxation from. Maybe, that was the problem. Summer was dragging on with not much to do. Erica was living with her dad in Denver for the summer and Whitney was working at Forever 21 and taking a summer school class.

"I'm bored," Story told Mom every day.

Mom would smile and say, "Why don't you call your friends, ride your bike, take a walk, or go to a museum?"

Story would shrug, leave the room, and find her cat, Maggie, who somehow understood her feelings of malaise. Story wasn't in the mood to do anything. Hanging up a top or folding shorts and putting them in a drawer seemed overwhelming to her.

The housekeeper was charged with cleaning every room, except the kids' rooms, because they were supposed to learn responsibility and clean their own. Betsy and Kimberly kept theirs spotless. But ever since she'd moved into Anthony's room, Story hadn't felt like putting anything back where it belonged. There was something about the freedom of her own space and her urge to rebel against her parents for a change that prevented her from doing anything they instructed her to do, or even what she thought she *should* do.

After the sitcom ended, she flipped the channels until she landed on a Lifetime movie about a girl who had run away from home and was trying to find something to eat. It reminded Story of that girl's diary she was reading. It was hard to relate to hunger. The problem at her house was that there was almost too much food.

A few years ago, there were a few days when they might not have fresh bread or fruit until Mom went to the grocery store. Then she'd hired Nina to do the shopping, cook dinner, and pack lunches for Story and her siblings. With fewer cooking responsibilities, Mom had put her energies into making a hot breakfast every morning and baking cookies, cupcakes, and pies from scratch. She was born in the 1950s when girls were taught to value homemaking, raising children, and taking care of their husbands. Her favorite show as a child had been *Leave It to Beaver,* and Story often teased her about her similarity to June Cleaver—the mother in the series.

It wasn't until a few months ago that Story could no longer button her pants and connected this with weight gained from what she called the "food bombardment." On the positive side, she talked Mom into a higher clothing allowance to buy bigger sizes. But, on the negative side, she hated her image even more in the mirror.

Sometimes, she thought that maybe she should do something to lose weight or make her life more interesting, but then another sitcom she liked would come on and she'd be temporarily transported away.

***

*August 3, 1993—9:35 P.M.*

Mrs. Hernandez suggested I write about my feelings in my diary, probably because I wouldn't stop crying. She was with a police officer when they showed Dad a court order to put me in foster care. I think he had taken some drugs, because he didn't put up much of a fight. His hands were shaking, and he kept glancing at the mattress on the floor.

I packed my clothes in the big suitcase. When I refused to leave, because of my library books, Dad promised to return them. I hugged him and he whispered, "You'll be back soon."

I'm not sure I believe him.

My foster parents are Jim and Nancy. They're both very fat and have a fat grown son, Mick, who plays video games and watches TV in their family room. They also have a fat, white cat named Cloud. I could smell the litter box when we walked into the house.

Mrs. Hernandez carried my suitcase to my new bedroom and tried to convince me to stop crying. She finally left. I think she was done with work.

The white cat jumped on my bed and I petted her until Nancy told me I had to set the table for dinner. She said

I had to do chores. I've never set a table before and so I didn't know what to do.

She sighed loudly, then showed me where the silverware goes next to the plates. We ate pot roast, mashed potatoes, gravy, green beans, rolls, and chocolate Bundt cake for dessert. I had two big glasses of milk. There was a lot of food and everyone took seconds until it was gone. The family seemed as hungry as I was, and no one talked while we ate. Everyone chewed loudly and clinked their silverware. I helped put dishes in the dishwasher after dinner, and then I said I was tired so I could go to my room.

My bedroom has a yellow quilt on the bed and green shag carpet. There are a few pictures on the walls with lakes and trees. There's even a dresser for my clothes.

I share a bathroom with Mick. It has soft toilet paper and lilac scented soap. I'm scared, but there's electricity, so I can sleep with the light on.

*August 4, 1993—8:45 P.M.*

Nancy gave me a long list of chores to do. I had to vacuum the house. I know how to sweep, but I've never used a vacuum before. It's heavy and loud. Nancy seemed annoyed when I asked her where to put the coins in the washer and dryer. We always had to go to a Laundromat or wash clothes in the sink. I know how to dust, but Nancy yelled at me when she saw me dust after I was done vacuuming.

"Are you stupid?" she asked.

I wanted to tell her that I'm a little girl and not a housekeeper, but I kept my mouth shut.

Jim left for work early in the morning and Nancy and Mick watched game shows on TV and ate chips. She told me to make my own lunch, so I had a ham and cheese sandwich, an apple, and a brownie. The refrigerator is so full, I had to move some jars around to find the mayonnaise.

While I was folding laundry, I smelled chicken frying in the kitchen and when I was sweeping the bathroom floor, I smelled cookies baking. Dinner was delicious.

Jim asked me if I had a nice first day in their home. I nodded and looked down. Maybe he doesn't know that I'm the new maid.

*August 8, 1993—9:10 P.M.*

Mrs. Hernandez came by today for a follow-up. In front of Nancy, I acted like everything was fine. When she came into my room to meet with me privately, I told her the truth. Mrs. Hernandez took notes while I told her the brilliant plan of how this family gets paid for having a live-in maid. She then put her notebook down and said to be patient. Nancy is probably trying to teach me responsibility and how to do chores. She explained to me that many parents require their children to do chores every day and there's nothing wrong with it.

After she left, Nancy yelled at me for leaving my yellow sweater on the couch and ordered me to scrub the toilets. I wonder if Mick had to clean when he was my age. I want to ask him, but every time I start to speak to him, he tells me to be quiet—he's in the middle of a game or show.

Tomorrow, I'm going to ask Nancy if I can go to the library. If she cares about me at all, how can she say no?

*August 10, 1993—7:34 P.M.*

Nancy said she'd take me to the library after I finished my chores yesterday. I never got done. I cleaned the oven, the refrigerator, and the barbeque grill. When I was finished, I was going to take a shower, but she said, "Where do you think you're going, young lady? You haven't vacuumed and washed the windows."

I knew I wasn't going to the library.

Today, I didn't get out of bed for breakfast. My muscles in my shoulders are sore from scrubbing and my back hurts from bending. I've been eating so much that my clothes are getting tight.

At 8:30, Nancy came into my room without knocking and told me to get up. I closed my eyes and ignored her until she pulled the blankets off the bed and I was lying on only the sheet. Cloud, the cat, was sleeping on my legs and I heard her run out of the room. I don't think the cat likes Nancy.

I told her I was sore from scrubbing and asked for a day off to go to the library. I thought she'd argue, but she said she would take me. She was going to stay there with me until I picked out some books, but I asked her to leave me there and pick me up before dinner.

She said she'd be back by 2:00. I had to do chores.

This was the best day I've had since I've been in foster care. I checked out 4 books. Hopefully, they'll last until I can talk her into taking me to the library again. I asked the librarian when school starts, and she said on August 23rd.

When I told Nancy, she rolled her eyes and said, "What are you going to do with an education?"

I hope Mrs. Hernandez comes back soon. I'm worried that Nancy won't let me go to school.

# Chapter Four

Whitney finally retuned Story's call during dinner. The "no phone calls during dinner" rule was probably the strictest of any her parents imposed. The only time it was violated was when there was an emergency. The family could hear the voicemail messages from the dining room table. They'd continue eating unless the person calling sounded frantic and labeled his or her call an emergency. Story could only remember two such calls—when her grandmother had died, and when Anthony had sustained a concussion from football practice.

After a meal of grilled salmon, corn on the cob, and sweet potato fries, Story headed to her room to call her friend. The best thing about having her own room was that Kimberly couldn't eavesdrop on her conversations anymore. There were five phones in the house—in each bedroom, except Betsy's, and one in the kitchen and one in the den. It wasn't until this summer that Story'd ever been able to have a private call.

"What's up?" she asked Whitney.

"I saw Neville at the mall today."

"Are you kidding me?" Story felt her stomach flutter. She'd had her eye on Matt Neville ever since he'd started attending their school mid-way sophomore year.

"I was folding jeans and saw him walk past with Mike and Justin."

"Oh, my God!" Story squealed.

"If you hung out at the mall like the other kids, you'd run into him."

Story nodded. "You're right. Maybe he'll be there again tomorrow."

"Maybe. If you had a job at the mall, you'd see everyone," Whitney said. "Last week, half the drill team came in and a few of the cheerleaders."

"Really?" Story was on the edge of being in the popular group at school. She was friendly with some of the girls, because they'd been friends in elementary and junior high school. She'd hoped her new car would increase her status, but now that she'd gained weight, she wasn't so sure.

"Tomorrow, I'm working the day shift. My lunch is at one. Come by and we can cruise."

"Definitely," Story said, and smiled.

After they hung up, she searched her bedroom floor for something to wear to the mall. She tried on pants until she found some jeans that fit. The cute purple top she'd bought a few weeks ago was still hanging in her closet with the tags on. It would be perfect.

***

*August 12, 1993—11:32 P.M.*

Jim and Nancy had a big fight tonight. I heard them yelling at each other and stomping around their room. It started with him complaining about his tuna salad sandwich in his lunch. She was sick of cooking dinner. Why didn't they ever go out to eat? After a few minutes, I was bored with their argument about food and went back to reading my book.

When I heard my name, I put the book down and listened. Jim said I broke the barbeque when I cleaned it. Nancy complained about how I don't know how to do even the simplest chores and I'm as slow as a snail. Maybe they don't know the walls are paper-thin and that I could hear everything they said.

After they criticized everything about me, Jim asked, "Can we trade her in for an older girl?"

Cloud was cuddled in bed with me and I pulled her close and cried into her fur. I'm not sure why I was crying. I hate this place.

*August 13, 1993 —8:55 P.M.*

They acted like the fight never happened. This morning, Jim took his tuna sandwich to work as usual and I was given a list of chores to do while Nancy and Mick watched a talk show. I don't know why I tried to work faster. It would be logical to work slower so they'd trade me in for a better housekeeper. Dad said I'm a people pleaser just like him. I miss him.

*August 15, 1993—9:30 P.M.*

Jim and Nancy went to a wedding today, so I had the house to myself, except for Mick. He was supposed to watch me, but he slept all day on the couch. I put a towel and swimsuit in my backpack and walked the neighborhood until I found a public swimming pool. It was family swim, so I was able to swim laps and relax in the water for over an hour. It's been ages since I've swam. It felt wonderful to stretch my body and feel weightless in the water.

When I got back to the house, Mick was still asleep, so I packed up my books and walked about three miles to the library. I checked out John Grisham's new book, *The Client* and *The Bridges of Madison County*. I didn't want to carry too many books back to the house, so I only got 3.

Mick was still sleeping, so I made myself a big salad for lunch. The lettuce and tomatoes were for burgers, but I was craving veggies. I think the only salad Nancy knows how to make is potato salad.

When Mick finally woke up, he cooked a frozen pizza for himself and ate the whole thing. I was upstairs, and he yelled at me to come down and wash his dishes. I did what I was told. If everything went well while Jim and Nancy were away, maybe they'd leave more often. I can only hope.

*August 18, 1993—8:43 P.M.*

I got in big trouble today. Nancy said she was spending the day shopping with a friend. She gave me a list of chores to do, and Mick was there to "keep an eye on" me. I finished the chores while Mick was asleep, so I snuck out to go swimming. When I returned a few hours later, Nancy and Mrs. Hernandez were waiting for me. I'm not sure what happened. Maybe Nancy's shopping trip was canceled. More likely—she'd planned this to get rid of me.

Summer is almost over, and school starts next week. I've finished all the big cleaning chores, so I'm not much use to her anymore. She said they had a foster child last summer, and I wonder if she used the same scheme.

Nancy said, "This isn't working out," to Mrs. Hernandez.

I nodded my head in agreement and asked, "Can I go home?"

Mrs. H seemed upset and said there weren't any other foster homes available, but she'd put me on the list. After she left, I didn't leave my room for dinner. This must have made Nancy mad, because I could hear her banging the plates and pans while she washed the dishes. There's no way I'm doing chores tomorrow. I'll find a way to sneak out of the house.

# Chapter Five

After Story picked out her outfit for the mall, she tossed a few dirty clothes into the hamper, hung up some tops, and folded a half-dozen pairs of jeans and shorts and placed them neatly in her drawers. It was almost midnight when she finished cleaning her room. She'd even put clean sheets on her bed while Maggie lay curled up on the heap of soiled sheets on the floor.

"You've got to move, kitty," Story said as she picked Maggie up and placed her on the foot of her bed.

She put the full hamper out in the hall for Lorissa, the housekeeper, who'd be there the next morning. Now that her room was neat, Story wished she could vacuum, but it was too late and everyone else was sleeping. Maybe she could talk Lorissa into vacuuming while she was at the mall the next day.

She changed into her pajamas and crawled into bed with her high school yearbook. She thumbed through the pages with most of the white spaces filled with her classmates' notes, from "have a great summer" to long remembrances of the previous year's highlights.

She turned to the page with Matt's school picture. He had wavy brown hair, blue sparkling eyes, and a dimple in his right cheek when he smiled. She then turned to the candid picture of him and a few other baseball players when they'd washed cars to raise funds for game travel. He'd written his name almost illegibly next to the picture and had written, "Story, it was nice getting to know you this year. I hope to hang out with you more next year and hear your stories. Ha! Get it?"

Matt wasn't the only one who referenced her nickname. Unlike the others, she hoped he truly wanted to spend time with her.

Last year, she'd gone to the homecoming dance with Trent Seligman, a boy from her history class, and had asked Tommy White to the Sadie Hawkins dance, because she'd heard he liked her. She'd made out with both boys after the dance until their parents had picked them up and drove her home.

Matt was a year older and drove a shiny, black Honda Civic. The only girl she'd seen him with was Joslyn, the cheerleader with the red hair, who everyone called Flame. Story hoped they'd broken up over the summer.

She reread what Matt had written, smiled, and closed her eyes with the light on and the open book resting on her chest.

***

*August 26, 1993—8:15 P.M.*

A lot has happened since I wrote last. I'm now living with the Kekoa family in Santa Clarita. They have 3 foster kids and 5 of their own kids, and so the house is packed with people. I share an upstairs room with a foster girl named Jillian and the two Kekoa girls, Haukea and Akela. The boys have their own room in the basement. Mr. and Mrs. Kekoa are very nice. They moved to California from Hawaii five years ago, because it was too expensive to raise a family there. We have to take our shoes off before we enter the front door and there's a huge pile of shoes at the entryway to the house. We eat rice and lots of weird food like poke, laulau, poi, chicken long rice, spam musubi, lomilomi salmon, manapua, loco moco, and saimin. I can't help much in the kitchen, because I've never seen this kind of food before. I like almost everything, but the poi is kind of gross. Mrs. Kekoa said not to eat it if I don't like it.

She doesn't make me do chores, but I help out anyway. I swept and vacuumed the house, did laundry, and cleaned the bathrooms and the kitchen on Sunday when the family went to church. The older boy, Kimo, stayed home too, because he has the flu.

I've never been to church before, so Mrs. Kekoa sat

down with me and said that I've gone through so many changes in my life that I could wait a few weeks before I joined them. When they got home and the house was clean, everyone hugged me or gave me a high five! I'm happy here. The only problem is that Mrs. Hernandez said this home is temporary and I'll have to leave in a few months.

*September 1, 1993—8:40 P.M.*

My new school is the best ever. Haukea is in my class and she's introduced me to her group of awesome friends. I've been mostly hanging out with Haukea, Amanda, Melissa, and Nicole. We make up cheers at recess and Amanda is teaching us how to do back handsprings and one-handed cartwheels. She takes gymnastics class after school. Haukea and Melissa are Girl Scouts. They meet on Wednesdays and want me to join. I want to, but I don't have money for any fees or the uniform. I told them I'd think about it. If something changes and I stay here longer, maybe I can make money doing chores or something.

My favorite thing is not having to be on the free breakfast and lunch program at school. Mrs. Kekoa feeds us hot oatmeal or cold cereal, or fried spam and bananas for breakfast. She makes lunches for all of us and puts them in brown paper bags. Today, I had a peanut butter and jelly sandwich, an apple, 3 Oreo cookies, and a juice box. She even put a folded napkin in the bag with a note that said, "Have a great day, Zana!"

Mr. Kekoa is nice, too. He asked me about a library book I was reading last night. When I told him about the story, he asked me questions and listened to my answers. I wish they were my real parents.

# Chapter Six

The alarm clock dinged, and Story pulled the covers over her head. *Five more minutes.*

"Sleepyhead, time to get up," Mom said from the doorway.

"No!"

"You have to eat a good breakfast on your first day back to school."

Story groaned, threw back the covers, and rubbed her eyes. She'd taken a shower the night before to save time. After brushing her long wavy black hair and pulling it into a ponytail, she washed her face and brushed her teeth, then stood in front of her closet in her underwear looking for something to wear that didn't make her look fat. She tried on three pairs of pants before deciding on dark blue jeans that barely buttoned and a black top.

Her mother surveyed her as she entered the kitchen. "Jeans on your first day?"

Story nodded as she took her seat at the table next to Betsy.

"Eat while it's hot." Her mother handed her a plate of fried eggs, sausage, and toast with jam.

Story took a bite of eggs, prepared in her second favorite way. She took a few bites of sausage and toast before pushing her plate away.

"There are starving children in China," her mother said as her dad walked in.

Story rolled her eyes. "Okay, send them my leftovers."

She'd never fit into her jeans if she ate everything, and Matt would never notice her. She'd been to the mall a handful of times, as suggested by Whitney, and had only caught sight of him from far away once. She hoped he'd be assigned a locker near hers, or maybe they'd run into each other between classes.

"There are plenty of kids starving in California." Her dad sat down at the kitchen table and opened the front section of the newspaper he was holding.

Story would have argued like she had the last time, but she remembered that girl's situation in the diary. She shrugged, pulled the plate closer, and ate two of the three sausage links and took a few bites of toast.

"That wasn't so bad, was it?" her mother said.

Story shook her head, picked up her plate, and put it in the sink. She started to say that she had to hurry to catch the bus, and then caught herself, smiled, and grabbed her keys off the counter.

"Wait. Can you drive your sisters to school today?" Mom asked.

"Can't they take the bus like always?" Story frowned and looked at her watch. She'd have to leave a half hour early if she took Kimberly to junior high and Betsy to elementary school. It was already too late.

"They could—"

"Mom, I'm going to be late as it is." She grabbed her keys and left without waiting for her mother to finish her sentence. There was no way she was going to become her sisters' personal chauffer and her parents' errand girl. She sighed deeply and pulled out of the driveway.

***

*September 6, 1993—8:20 P.M.*

I had a fight with Junior. I don't think I mentioned him before. He's the Kekoa's thirteen-year-old son. His name is James like his dad, but everyone calls him Junior. We had a Labor Day barbeque in the backyard with some neighbor families. The kids were playing on a Slip N Slide.

I took a running start and went so fast, I crashed into Junior as he was getting up at the end. He didn't say much, but then went into the house for a while. After playing on the slide, I was talking with one of the neighbor girls, Andrea, who's in Junior's class. She kept looking at him, so I asked her if she liked him.

She smiled and looked down but didn't say anything.

Later, I took a big piece of chocolate cake into the kitchen to eat. Junior was the only one in there, and he yelled at me for being a pig and hogging all the cake. He said I'm a moocher and should go back to Compton or wherever I came from.

I don't know what his problem is, but Mr. Kekoa came in and heard some of what his son said. I took my cake and went back outside.

Later, Mr. Kekoa asked me if I liked living with them. I said I do very much, and thanked him for everything.

He said that he's a family law attorney and when he goes to court, sometimes the social workers tell him about a child who desperately needs a foster home. That's how he heard about me. He said he could provide me a home for a few months while they look for a more permanent foster family. He asked me if I knew that I would soon be leaving.

I said I did, but that I wished I could stay.

He smiled with his mouth, but his eyes looked kind of watery. He patted me on the shoulder and suggested I stay clear of Junior. As he walked away, he shook his head and muttered, "Teenagers."

*September 11, 1993—9:00 P.M.*

We went swimming at a public pool today. The whole Kekoa family went, except for Junior. He had soccer practice. Everyone played in the pool while I swam laps. It felt good after not swimming for a month. Afterwards, Mrs. Kekoa raved about what a great swimmer I am and said she'd look into finding a swim team I can join. I couldn't stop smiling.

Later, at the dinner table, Mr. Kekoa asked if I had any other hidden talents. Mom taught me not to brag, so I wasn't sure how to answer. I told them about sewing almost all of my clothes and modeling in some department store fashion shows with Mom.

Mrs. Kekoa said I could use her sewing machine anytime I wanted to. I'm so excited, because I need to let the seams out of some of my clothes to make them fit.

I can also alter some of Mom's clothes that I have with me. I don't have money for fabric or patterns, so I'll have to work with the clothes I have. On the bright side, I'm changing schools so much that no one has seen my old clothes.

*September 13, 1993—8:45 P.M.*

Junior yelled at me this morning because I left my shoes in the entryway instead of outside. I've been trying to avoid him, but he seems to pop up everywhere. He even complained after I vacuumed the entire house. He said I'm trying to brownnose his parents. I don't even know what that means, but I think it's bad. I ignored him and cleaned the bathrooms.

*September 18, 1993—8:40 P.M.*

Mrs. Kekoa took me shopping today at J.C. Penney's. She bought me 2 pairs of shoes, jeans, black pants, a sweater, and underwear. We then went to a fabric store and she bought me fabric, patterns, and notions so I can make my own tops and dresses.

I had tears rolling down my cheeks when I hugged her and then I thanked her.

She told me the state gives her money to take care of me and she takes her responsibility very seriously.

I asked, "You mean Nancy and Jim got money to take care of me, too?"

She said, "Yes sweetie, that's how it works."

I'm so pissed. I begged Nancy for new shoes. She said I was too much of a burden financially for her to buy me anything, that I was lucky to be fed and have a roof over my head.

*September 19, 1993—8:25 P.M.*

I went to church for the very first time this morning.

Before we went, Mrs. Kekoa explained to me that her family was from the Philippines and were Catholic. She and her parents moved to Hawaii when she was ten years old, and they went to mass every day. She met Mr. Kekoa in church when she was a teenager. He's a mixture of Hawaiian, Chinese, Filipino, and Irish. They married in a Catholic church when she was eighteen years old and he was twenty-one. I think that's why they have crosses with Jesus on them and pictures of Jesus all over the house. Everyone in the family wears a cross necklace.

At church, it was quiet except for organ music. Everyone sang songs and repeated words written in books. There was a lot of kneeling and standing up. I found it all confusing.

Mom was a Lutheran when she was a kid. Dad called himself an atheist and wouldn't let me go to church with friends on the few occasions they'd asked. Mom seemed fine with not going to church. She and Dad always went for a long run or bike ride on Sundays when there wasn't a race. I'm not sure I like church, but it doesn't seem as bad as Dad described it. I might go again.

# Chapter Seven

Story hoped her parents had gone to bed, but no such luck. All the downstairs lights were on, making it impossible to sneak in. She was chewing gum, hoping they didn't smell her breath. She opened the door quietly and started up the stairs.

"Where do you think you're going, young lady?" Mom demanded.

Story turned and said, "Oh, hey. I didn't see you there. Goodnight!"

Dad tapped his watch.

"Sorry. It's only eleven-fifteen." Story joined them in the living room.

"It's eleven-thirty," Mom said.

"The movie went longer than I thought, and then Erica wanted to get something to eat." Story said the well-rehearsed lines she'd practiced on the way home. She tried her best to act normal.

Mom raised an eyebrow.

"Next time you're late, you'll be grounded," Dad said.

Mom rose to give her a hug. "Get to bed. We have church in the morning."

Usually, Story protested about going to church, but didn't want to press her luck. Besides, she'd just read in Zana's diary that she didn't grow up going to church. Maybe it wasn't so bad.

Back in her room, she immediately changed into her pajamas and went to the bathroom to brush her teeth in case her parents decided to further investigate her movie story. She still felt a bit tipsy and smiled at having walked normally into the house and up the stairs. It was Whitney who had warned her not to drink more than two beers at the keg. Since Erica had driven, Story thought she should have been able to drink as much as she'd wanted.

But Whitney was right. Had she been totally wasted, she would've gotten into more trouble and might have acted even more foolishly when Matt had asked her about her summer.

She'd spotted him the moment he'd showed up at the party with a few guys from the baseball team. Joslyn had also been at the party but seemed to be solely interested in a football player from another high school.

Story had pulled her ponytail out of the elastic band and let her long curls fall loose, then positioned herself near the snacks table where Matt and his friends were talking.

"I did all sorts of fun things," she'd said, describing her summer in response to his question.

"Like what?"

"Oh, you know. Beach, travel, relax." She'd felt her face flush, hoping he wouldn't question her further.

"Sounds like fun," he'd said, and swigged beer from a red Solo cup.

She would've asked him about his summer if her brain hadn't felt like mush.

Instead, he'd asked, "Are you going out for any sports this fall?"

"Sure. What about you?"

"I'm trying out for the swim team on Monday." He'd grinned with his wide dimpled smile. "Last year I played football, but I need to avoid getting injured before baseball season. Swimming is good for conditioning."

Story had nodded.

"What sport are you doing?"

"Swimming, too." The words had flown out of her mouth before she could stop them.

Matt had smiled, then turned to join his friends' beer pong game.

"Shit!" Story had said after she'd found Erica in an adjacent room. "I told Matt I'm trying out for the swim team."

"Are you serious?"

Story had nodded.

It had been a few years since she was on her neighborhood swim team, and she'd never been serious about it or competitive. How could she possibly try out and make the team without making a complete fool out of herself?

"I guess you'll have to practice." Erica had laughed.

Story had frowned and bitten her lip.

***

*September 23, 1993—8:45 P.M.*

I'm really freaked out right now. Dad showed up at my swim practice and was yelling my name. He was super skinny, his pants were dirty and torn, and even though I was in the water, I could smell him when he walked into the pool area. I didn't know what to do so I kept swimming laps until the coach blew his whistle and told us to stop.

At first, I thought maybe everyone would think Dad was a crazy homeless guy, but he started wailing and saying I'm his daughter and that I was stolen from him. All the other kids stared at me. I wanted to die. Coach Brian told him to leave, or he'd call the police.

I think Dad was on drugs, because he ignored Brian and staggered towards the pool. I'm not sure if he saw me before the security guards grabbed his arms and took him away.

Coach Kerri told me to get out of the water. She wrapped me in a towel and took me to the locker room where she put her arm around me while I sobbed uncontrollably. I don't know how he found me. Mrs. Hernandez had assured me that he wouldn't know who I was placed with or where I was living. I'm not exactly scared of him, but it's embarrassing. I wish I was a normal kid with normal parents. I wish Mom was here.

*September 24, 1993—9:45 P.M.*

I wouldn't get out of bed today. Mrs. Kekoa felt my forehead and took my temperature. She finally put her hands on her hips and said my sickness had to be in my head. She sat down on the bed and held my hand for a long time. I finally told her what happened at the pool. I'm afraid that if I go to school, Dad will show up.

Since I'm so far ahead in my schoolwork, Mrs. Kekoa let me take a sick day and spend the day sewing a dress. In the afternoon, Miss Creighton, who's taken over my Child Protective Services case from Mrs. Hernandez, came by to meet with us about my case. She doesn't know how Dad found out about my swim practice. She asked me if I had any ideas.

I didn't want her to know that my hands were shaking and sweat was running down my back. I stared at the loose threads on the hem of her dress. I wanted to offer to cut them off, but I whispered that I knew one of the girls on swim team, Kiki Green, who I used to swim with in Ventura. Maybe Kiki told her parents or someone who knows Dad.

Miss Creighton said that soon I'll be placed with a family in Thousand Oaks after one of their foster kids ages out of the system.

I kicked the coffee table and said no so loudly, I startled myself.

Mrs. Kekoa came over and hugged me tightly.

"I want to stay here," I screamed.

I noticed the two women exchange looks. Finally, Miss Creighton left.

*September 27, 1993—8:30 P.M.*

I wore my new dress today. I sewed all weekend, and by Sunday afternoon, it was finished. Mrs. Kekoa pretended to like it, but I know she doesn't get the fashion. The grunge look is in, so I made a red plaid baby doll dress. The kids at school loved it and some of the popular girls came up to me and asked where I'd bought it.

When I told them I'd made it myself, they asked me to make them one, too. I nodded politely, but I don't think my foster parents will let me use their house as a dress making shop. Anyways, I have to spend every moment possible using the sewing machine while I can for my own clothes, because I'll soon be moving to Thousand

Oaks. Another CPS abduction is in the works. I'll wake up one morning and they'll give me 30 minutes to pack my suitcase, then I'll be off to live with another strange family. In the meantime, anytime I'm not sewing, I'm cleaning and helping Mrs. Kekoa. Maybe she won't want me to leave.

*October 1, 1993—9:50 P.M.*

Mr. Kekoa suggested I return to swim practice. I think he wants to get me out of the house. All the other kids have after school and weekend sports or scouts' activities, but I'm always home.

I told him I'll start back on Monday. I don't think Dad will be there, and I'll do anything to make the Kekoas like me. Junior stuck his tongue out at me this morning and called me a brownnoser.

I laughed and asked him if I could clean his room. He rolled his eyes.

*October 9, 1993—8:05 P.M.*

I got an A++ on my writing assignment. I decided not to show it to the Kekoas, because their kids' grades are in the B range. I think Junior gets Cs and Ds. His dad is always telling him he can't watch TV until he does better.

I like school, but it's so easy. I can get my homework done in less than an hour. I've used up all the fabric Mrs. Kekoa bought for me, and I'm almost done with altering my clothes, so I read library books while the other kids study.

Mr. Kekoa noticed how much I like to read and lets me pick out books from the shelves in his den. He has a lot of books about family law.

I started to read one, but I didn't understand much, so I read one of his John Grisham novels instead.

## Chapter Eight

Mrs. Blanchard paused by Story's desk as she handed back her history quiz, which she'd folded. Story noticed that her teacher hadn't folded any of the other quizzes. Her stomach churned as she peeked at her grade. A large red D+ was written at the top of the page, which was heavily marked with matching pen. She'd gotten almost all the questions wrong.

Although Story wasn't honor roll material, she'd never received a grade below a C before. The rest of the class was a blur as she tried to figure out what to do. Her parents would probably find out. Would they kick her off the swim team? She'd been practicing hard and had just barely made the cut. But, it was worth it to see Matt every day after school. Sometimes, he'd pause before getting into his car and talk to her for a few minutes. Mostly, he talked about the workout or the upcoming meet.

After her parents shook their heads in disapproval about her grade, Mom said, "I think you should quit swim team and focus on your schoolwork."

"No, Mom. It's not because of swimming," Story explained.

"What's the problem, then?"

"The first section of history was boring. Mrs. Blanchard said our next section will address historical women's issues. It should be more exciting."

"I don't want to get another call from the vice principal's office," Mom said with her hands on her hips. She gave Dad a look, then turned to Story and sighed loudly. "Do you promise to apply yourself?"

Story nodded vigorously. "Absolutely. I'll go up to my room and study right now."

After a long pause, Mom said, "Okay."

Story raced up the stairs, grabbed her history book, and read about World War II and the Holocaust. After a half hour, she ran downstairs for a glass of milk and some Oreos. She clicked on the TV while she ate her snack and as soon as she was done, turned it off. However, instead of returning to history, she opened Zana West's diary and began reading where she'd left off the night before.

*October 11, 1993—9:40 P.M.*

Jillian left today, because her mother is now out of rehab. They're going to live at her grandmother's house. Like me, Jillian loves the Kekoa family and she was scared to leave. She confided in me one night that her mother is a cocaine addict and has lots of boyfriends. One of them came into her room when she was sleeping. She didn't tell me any details, but it sounded scary. I asked Jillian about her grandmother, and she said she has a bad temper and will spank her if she doesn't do everything perfectly.

Maybe now that Jillian's gone, there's room for me to stay. No one has told me the reason why I can't stay here permanently. I asked Haukea if she knows, and she said it might have something to do with Junior, but she's not sure.

*Friday, October 15, 1993—9:00 P.M.*

We carved pumpkins after school today. I watched the others, because I didn't know what to do. Junior laughed when I said I'd never done it before. My face turned red and I was going to leave the room. And then, Mrs. Kekoa told him to shush. My parents were either racing in an Ironman triathlon or a marathon this time of year, so we didn't do much to celebrate Halloween.

A few years ago, Mom bought 3 tiny pumpkins and I drew faces on them with a black marking pen. That was a fun day. I miss Mom.

Haukea moved her pumpkin next to mine and showed me what to do. I was the last to finish, but my pumpkin has a big grin and triangle eyes. Mr. Kekoa said it's a beauty. I was going for scary.

*Sunday, October 17, 1993—8:50 P.M.*

After church today, we had brunch to celebrate Junior's 14th birthday. His grandparents, aunts, uncles, and cousins came over and everyone brought food and gifts. I don't have any money, so I made him a card with construction paper. I used the rest of my plaid material to make him a book bag. He startled me with a pat on the back and a smile after he opened my gift.

*Saturday, October 26, 1993—9:20 P.M.*

Mrs. Kekoa gave me some black fabric to make a witch costume. She didn't give me a pattern, so I used some patterns from other dresses. It sort of looks like a black baby doll dress. I can't fix it, because I need to save material for the hat. The other kids have store-bought costumes. Haukea said I can use her leftover green face makeup from last year. Since my hair is black, I won't need a wig.

*Monday, October 28, 1993—8:30 P.M.*

I can't wait until Halloween. I was able to make a pointy hat with thin cardboard and covered it with black material. I made the hem of my dress ragged and found an old broom in the garage.

Mr. Kekoa is taking us trick or treating while Mrs. Kekoa hands out little candy bars to kids who come to the house.

I've only been trick or treating once—when I was six years old. I dressed like a swimmer, because my parents didn't have money to buy me a real costume. We only went to about 5 houses and I shared my M&Ms and candy corn with Dad and Mom.

*Wednesday, October 30, 1993—9:05 P.M.*

I don't know if I'm going to be able to sleep tonight. I'm so excited about Halloween. Haukea said we get to fill pillowcases with candy, and we can keep anything that doesn't have razor blades in it. It will last for a long time, because I'm going to eat only 1 piece each day. I have a feeling it's going to be one of the best days of my life.

*Thursday, October 31, 1993—8:25 P.M.*

I'm totally bummed. When I got home from school, the other kids and I were getting ready for trick-or-treating when the phone rang. While on the phone, Mrs. Kekoa was crying. Then, Mr. Kekoa came home. They told us to go downstairs and watch TV in the basement and not open the door to Trick-or-Treaters. They said we could eat the candy in the plastic pumpkin bucket that was meant for the trick-or-treaters while they were gone.

Hours later, they came home. Mrs. Kekoa went straight to her room and Mr. Kekoa told us that Junior had gotten drunk, stolen a car, and crashed it. He broke his nose and some ribs, and had a head injury from the accident. He was in the hospital, but would probably go to a boys' detention home when he got better.

Haukea asked her dad a question, but he turned around and went to his bedroom without answering her.

I washed the green makeup off my face, but I'm sleeping in my witch's dress.

*Saturday, November 2, 1993—9:15 P.M.*

I haven't seen Mrs. Kekoa since Halloween. Mrs. Dempsey from next door came over with some food for dinner last night and stayed until we went to bed. I spent the day reading library books in my room until Mr. Kekoa asked me to come into his den for a talk. He told me that Junior had a seizure and is in intensive care at the hospital. The kids are going to be staying with their grandparents, but they don't have room for me. I'm going to be staying at Mrs. Dempsey's until Monday morning and then Child Protective Services will be taking me to a new home.

I tried not to cry in front of Mr. Kekoa. His hands were shaking and he looked like he hadn't slept in days. He hugged me and whispered good-bye.

# Chapter Nine

Story, Kimberly, and Betsy followed Mom down the basement stairs, through the seldom-used rec room complete with ping pong and pool tables, both covered to protect them from dust. The family converged downstairs a half dozen times each year, but otherwise used the large family room with its sixty-inch TV on the second floor instead. Beyond the rec room were a guest room, a bathroom, and an adjacent room they called “the closet” where there were floor-to-ceiling racks with ill-fitting or outdated clothes discarded by every member of the family.

They made a beeline to the lower rack on the left side of the room, where Halloween costumes of previous years were stored. The collection had grown so large that Mom had suggested that before they went shopping for costumes, they checked to see if there were some items they wished to recycle.

“OMG!” Kimberly squealed. She was holding a gumball machine costume that Story had worn when she was her age.

“You should totally wear that,” Story said.

Kimberly nodded and pulled it on over her long t-shirt and leggings.

“What’s this?” Betsy held up a bat costume.

“I think that was Anthony’s,” Kimberly said.

Story skipped the kid’s costumes and thumbed through her mom’s old costumes. She held up something that had a bodice and a short skirt with ruffles.

“What’s this, Mom?” she asked.

“My old Spanish sexy pirate dress.” Mom blushed. “I’m sure there’s something more appropriate here.”

“I like this,” Story said. She undressed and slipped the dress over her hips. It was a bit too snug.

"You look better in it than I did," Mom said. "But it isn't appropriate for your age."

"Mom, I can't zip this up," Betsy whined.

While Mom was distracted with the bat costume, Story searched the adjacent dresser drawers and found a hot pink corset, black stockings, long fingerless gloves, a hat with a pink feather, and a black choker. She grabbed a vampire cape and some fangs. When she had what she wanted, she dashed up the stairs before her mother could suggest a more modest costume.

Everyone who was anyone at her school was invited to John Scheland's Halloween party. Matt had mentioned it after swim practice, and Erica and Whitney were debating whether to dress in matching Catwoman costumes. They would ride in Whitney's VW Passat, because her parents made no restrictions on her driving with other kids in the car.

As planned, Story put on her mother's sexy pirate dress. She'd only eaten carrot sticks and apples for a few days, hoping it would zip up. It did—just barely.

She covered it up with the vampire cape and inserted the rubber fangs just before she left for the evening.

"Let me see," Mom asked, and then nodded with approval. "You look like a cute vampire."

"Yeah. Where's your scary blood and white make up?" Betsy asked.

"I can help you," Kimberly joined in.

"No, that's okay. That makeup gives me zits." Story smiled and headed out just as the doorbell rang. "I'll get this one." She grabbed the plastic Jack-O-Lantern bowl and doled out mini Snickers bars to a mermaid, two Harry Potters, a Superman, and a tiny blond police officer.

Whitney and Erica were waiting for her, and as they drove to the party, Story took out her vampire fangs and pulled off the cape, revealing her sexy costume.

Her friends approved, but Erica motioned for her to pull up the corset a bit. They could hear music from John's house from down the street where they'd parked. Trick-or-treaters dashed from house to house with their parents in tow. The porch was illuminated with a few Jack-O-Lanterns, but otherwise, the house was dark. Spiders, bats, and skeletons decorated the entranceway, which was already filled with people. The place was packed with kids wearing costumes and holding red Solo cups filled with beer.

They greeted their friends and marveled over each other's costumes. The girls had decided against Catwoman in favor of witches—Whitney was the good witch and Erica was the wicked witch.

"Where are John's parents?" Story asked. She'd only been to a few other parties with beer and could hardly fathom how he'd been able to manage this one.

"They're out of town on business. He's almost eighteen," Erica said. "I guess they trust him."

They sipped beer and listened to the blaring 3 Doors Down music when Matt approached, dressed as a pirate.

"Hey, what are you supposed to be?" he asked.

"A sexy pirate," Story said. His focus was on her cleavage.

"Nice." He smiled broadly.

The girls were engrossed in conversations with other classmates, leaving Story alone with Matt. They drank beer and commented on costumes, giving scores from 1-10.

"She definitely deserves a nine," he said, gesturing to a girl in a flapper costume.

"Maybe a seven." She laughed. "He gets a ten." She pointed to their classmate, Brad, wearing a fake muscle t-shirt.

"Oh, he does, does he?" Matt reached out and pulled Story towards him and surprised her with a soft kiss on the lips.

***

*Sunday, November 21, 1993—6:45 P.M.*

I thought I lost you, Diary. You were in a box I packed when I left the Kekoas' house but hadn't opened yet. I'm now living in Thousand Oaks with the McKee family. Mrs. McKee is nervous all the time and can barely leave the house, because she might get in an accident. Mr. McKee is never home, because it probably stresses him out to be with his wife. Celia, their seventeen-year-old daughter, is a Goth anorexic, if you can imagine what that looks like. She stays in her room a lot and her door has a picture of a coffin on it. I can pretty much do what I want as long as I listen to Mrs. McKee's warnings about looking both ways before I cross the street and take the vitamins she gives me.

All the kids at school know each other and have no interest in me, the new girl. The school has a decent library and I can check out 4 books at a time. I haven't found a swimming pool, but there's a bike in the garage that Mrs. McKee lets me ride if I wear a helmet. I've been riding all over the neighborhood in the afternoon. I'm thinking about trying to get a paper route. I could use some money. I doubt Mrs. McKee will let me spend any of the money she gets from the state for me. When I asked her for $5.00 for the class field trip to the California Museum of Art, she said she doesn't have that kind of money. I'm too embarrassed to tell my teacher that I can't go.

*Thanksgiving, November 25, 1993—7:55 P.M.*

A bunch of the McKees' relatives came over today for Thanksgiving. I don't remember a lot of their names, but they seemed more normal and friendlier than Mr. and Mrs. McKee and Celia. Mrs. McKee spent most of the day talking to her sister, Gwen. I overheard her tell Gwen that Celia will be leaving for Miami soon to attend a tattooing and body piercing school.

Gwen hugged her sister and said she was worried about her having an "empty nest." Mrs. McKee smiled and said she had planned in advance by getting a foster child. She talked about me like she had bought me at the grocery store.

*Wednesday, December 1, 1993—9:25 P.M.*

I wonder if it's possible to die of boredom. I've spent most of my time lying on my bed lately. I don't feel like reading, biking, or doing homework. Mrs. McKee's squeaky voice is grating on my nerves. I want to shake Celia to put some life into her. She stares at her plate at dinner without eating anything, then walks to her room like a zombie. I don't try to talk to anyone anymore. I'm not interested in them and they sure aren't interested in me.

## Chapter Ten

Story stared at her plate for a few minutes before pushing the string beans around. She took a small bite of chicken and pressed the mashed potatoes flat.

She hadn't felt like eating for days. Matt had stopped calling her a few days before she saw him with his arm around Tara, the new girl who had huge boobs and talked in a fake, sugary-sweet southern drawl.

Story couldn't imagine how her life could get any worse, and then she'd gotten her history test back. Another D. Her parents took away the keys to her car and removed the TV from her room until she got her grades up.

"Can I be excused?" she asked.

Her parents exchanged looks before Mom said, "Yes."

She took her plate to the kitchen and scraped the food into the garbage can. In her room, she read a few entries in Zana's diary before opening her history book. She decided to read it from the beginning to make up for not doing any of the homework all semester.

*Friday, December 10, 1993—7:18 P.M.*

A man from Child Protective Services stopped by today to tell us that Dad is trying to get me back. Mrs. McKee became hysterical. I don't know what to think. I'm desperate to leave this place, but at least there's food to eat, electricity, and hot water.

*Sunday, December 12, 1993—8:15 P.M.*

Mr. and Mrs. McKee were gone for a few hours today. I made sure Celia was in her room before I filled my backpack with food from the kitchen. I have cans of beans, corn, and fruit cocktail, a box of instant oatmeal, a few energy bars, and some beef jerky. I still have a few cans of spam I got from the Kekoas' house. I've stashed the food in a box in the back of my closet and put some clothes on top so no one will know about it. If I have to move back in with Dad, I'll at least have some food.

*Wednesday, December 14, 1993—9:10 P.M.*

I wish there was a hem on my pants to bring down. I must have grown another inch, because all of my pants are too short and a few kids have commented that they're high waters. If I had boots, I could hide their length. I'm by far the tallest girl in my class and am often asked if I'm on the basketball team. The girls' basketball coach suggested that I try out for the team next year. I told him, "Maybe." I hope I've moved in with a better family by then. I don't want to make any promises. Besides, I don't want to tell him that I don't know how to play basketball.

*Friday, December 16, 1993—8:05 P.M.*

We're now on winter break from school, so I'm stuck in the house until early January. While riding my bike, I found a public library a few miles away and there's a community pool I could go to if I could come up with some money. I'm going to ask Mrs. McKee if I can get a pool membership as a Christmas gift. That's all I want… and some new pants.

*Thursday, December 23, 1993—7:55 P.M.*

I've been back with Dad since Tuesday. He wouldn't give me very many details, but he promised he's changed and everything is going to be better. He moved to a one-bedroom apartment closer to the beach. It's a lot cleaner, and there's a fold-out couch in the living room instead of a dirty mattress on the floor. He got a job at a used car dealership working during the day. The best thing is there's food in the kitchen and he made a big salad for dinner. The second best thing is that I don't ever have to see Mrs. McKee again.

*Saturday, December 25, 1993—9:45 P.M.*

Merry Christmas! Dad was wearing a Santa Claus hat this morning. We don't have a Christmas tree or any decorations, but he did give me a few gifts he said were from Ole Saint Nick. He said I could open them after breakfast, which was scrambled eggs, hash browns, and toast.

I couldn't wait to open my presents and couldn't stop smiling. He gave me new swim goggles, a cap, swimsuit, and running shoes. I'm so excited! Dad wants me to start training for a kid's triathlon, and he said he'll train with me. He used to have muscles, but now he's super skinny, looks pale, and walks with a slight limp. I hope he can get back in shape.

*Tuesday, December 28, 1993—8:40 P.M.*

I ran around the neighborhood today and then went to the library for some new books. I read *The Christmas Box* by Richard Paul Evans. I cried when I finished it, because it's about the importance of family. I miss Mom.

# Chapter Eleven

Story's head was buried in her history book when her mom gave a light tap on the door and walked into her room.

"You don't need to pretend to read history anymore—your test is over."

"I like it," Story said without looking up. She was telling the truth. Once she began reading about history, her curiosity got the best of her. She wanted to learn and understand more about Prohibition, the Great Depression, and World War II. She became curious about the Civil War and had asked her parents if they could rent the video, *Gone with the Wind.* The family had spent a Saturday afternoon watching it and Story even wrote a paper about it for extra credit. Now, history was her favorite subject.

Mom smiled. "We're decorating the tree. Do you want to join us?"

Story nodded and placed the book face down on her bed. She'd finish the chapter on the Korean War later.

Christmas music was playing downstairs and Kimberly and Betsy were already hanging ornaments. Story grabbed a few colored balls and breathed in the scent of the Douglas fir before finding the perfect place for each. She worked wordlessly and soon had finished by putting the angel on the top of the tree.

They all stood back while Mom turned the living room light off and Dad plugged in the tree lights. Betsy and Kimberly clapped their hands and squealed at its beauty. Mom retreated and returned with cups of non-alcoholic eggnog for each of them to enjoy before they moved into the dining room for the Christmas Eve dinner that Nina had been cooking all day.

Story dove into the roast beef and mashed potatoes and

gravy—the first meal she'd felt like eating in weeks. Her jeans now felt loose around her waist and she had finally stopped ruminating over Matt.

She felt her cat, Maggie, rubbing against her leg. The only thing missing was her brother, Anthony. He'd gone with his girlfriend to her parents' house in Tennessee for Christmas but planned to fly home for a few days at New Year's while Brooke returned to Florida for work.

After they cleared away the dishes, Mom asked, "Who wants pie?"

They all raised their hands and giggled. Story ate small pieces of pecan and pumpkin pie—her favorites.

It was Betsy who asked, "Can we open one present tonight?"

"Have you been good?" Mom asked.

They all nodded.

Story noticed that her dad had left the room after he finished his pie. She knew what would happen next.

Santa appeared in the doorway and said, "Ho, ho, ho!"

The girls ran to him and followed as he entered the living room. First, Betsy sat on his lap and he pulled out a rectangle box wrapped in silver and gold paper. She shook it and then tore off the paper.

"Barbie!" She jumped off Santa's lap to play with her new toy.

Kimberly was next. Her present was a pink sweater—her favorite color.

Story wondered what her presents would be. She had been in such a dark mood in the weeks leading up to Christmas that every time she was asked what she wanted, she shrugged.

"Come sit on my lap, young lady," Santa beckoned.

She did as he asked and looked into her dad's kind eyes.

"Santa knows you've been sad lately. I hope this gift will cheer you up." He handed her a small box.

She didn't shake it, because she knew it must be a necklace or bracelet. She held it in her hand until Santa urged her to open it.

She finally tore off the paper and lifted the lid. It was her car keys.

***

*Friday, December 31, 1993—10:15 P.M.*

Dad went out with some friends to celebrate New Year's Eve. Ever since I've been back home with him, he's spent all his off work time at home. We don't have bikes anymore, but we've been swimming and running together. He makes dinner for me and we both do chores. Other than that, he watches TV and I read library books. I thought we'd do the same tonight, but he said that since it's New Year's Eve, he's going out to celebrate with friends. I asked him if that was a good idea since he hasn't been out of rehab very long. He told me not to worry and he'd be home no later than 1 A.M.

I'm sick of reading, so I'm watching a New Year's Eve show. I'm bored, but it's better than living at a foster home. If Dad can keep his job, everything will be good. Hopefully, 1994 will be a much better year.

*Saturday, January 1, 1994—10:50 A.M.*

Happy New Year! Sort of. Dad's not home yet. My stomach hurts.

*1:15 P.M.*

He's still not home. I took some Tums, but I'm still not feeling well. I walked around the neighborhood, because I could no longer concentrate on reading. I came back, hoping Dad would be home. No sign of him. I'm going to stay home until he gets here. When he gets home, I'm going to yell at him.

*8:35 P.M.*

Dad is still not home. I'm lying on the bed with only my lamp on. I didn't bother to turn on any lights or eat anything for dinner. This was the day I was going to make

New Year's Resolutions. I wanted a do-over, but it's not looking like that can happen. Dad wouldn't stay away this long unless he was using drugs again or if he had some sort of accident.

*Sunday, January 2, 1994—3:30 P.M.*

He stumbled home and passed out on the couch. There are fresh needle marks on his arm.

*Wednesday, January 5, 1994—8:05 P.M.*

My new school is okay. I know a few kids who also moved neighborhoods. Ashley still goes to my old school, and I heard that Jessica moved out of state. A few weeks ago, I took the bus to my old neighborhood to see my friends. I knocked on Jessica's door and a woman answered and said Jessica's family no longer lives there. She thinks they moved to New Mexico.

When I was walking towards Ashley's house, I saw her and a group of girls from my old school practicing cheerleading on her front lawn. They were laughing and they all wore cute clothes. I was wearing too-short pants and an old floral top that was missing 2 buttons. The bottom of my shoe has come apart, so it flaps when I walk. I've been cutting my own bangs, so they're sort of crooked. My heart was racing when I turned around and ran a few blocks to the bus stop. I hope they didn't see me.

## Chapter Twelve

Story had never made a New Year's Resolution before, but when she read that Zana had planned to make some, she found an empty school notebook and began her list.

*Story Sanchez's 2001 New Year's Resolutions*

1. Lose 5 more pounds.
2. Join a club or sport that Matt isn't involved in.
3. Keep my room clean.
4. Get Bs in my classes (As would be okay, too!)
5. Stay out of trouble.
6. Find a NICE boyfriend.
7. Stop thinking about Matt.
8. Stop talking about Matt.

She felt a pit in her stomach when she wrote his name down. The last time she'd written his name was on the back of her school notebook. She'd experimented with Story + Matt, Stephanie + Matt, and Matt + Story. She'd even written Story Neville and Matt and Stephanie Neville. Shortly after she'd seen him with another girl, she'd ripped off the back of her notebook and put it through the shredder. She'd then asked her mom to buy her another notebook.

"Story, the phone is for you," Kimberly yelled from down the hall.

She hadn't heard it ring. "I've got it," Story yelled back, hoping her sister would hang up the other phone rather than listen in.

"Hello."

"Hey you," Erica said. "Whit and I are going to watch fireworks on the beach, do you want to come?"

"Who's going to be there?" Story asked.

"Everyone."

Story knew who "everyone" was. All the popular kids—cheerleaders, football players, and everyone who hung out with them, including Matt and whatever girl he was with. There was no way she was going to watch them kiss at midnight.

"I can't make it," Story said.

"Are you for real? Everyone's going to be there."

"I have to stay with Betsy while my parents are out tonight," Story said. It wasn't quite the truth. Her parents were going out, but the next-door neighbor lady, Kathy with all the cats, was coming over to keep an eye on things (she would leave her cats at home). Story's parents had made it clear that she wasn't allowed to drive or ride in another car with a minor driving on New Year's Eve. If she did anything, it would be by taxi only. She wanted to spare her friend the details of these restrictions.

"You can get out of it," Erica said. "Can't Kimberly babysit?"

"They don't think she's old enough yet." Another truth.

"We'll miss you."

"Yeah, I'm bummed." Again, she was telling the truth. She wanted more than anything to hang out with her friends. But, how could she have fun if she kept looking for Matt all night, and especially if he were with another girl?

After hanging up the phone, she added another resolution to her list:

> 9. Pretend that Matt has fallen off the face of the Earth.

She smiled after she wrote it. This was the only way

she was going to function tonight and each and every day thereafter.

***

*Saturday, January 8, 1994—9:15 P.M.*

I think the woman in the living room is Dad's girlfriend. They're whispering and giggling, then it's quiet for minutes at a time. He hasn't been home much this week. Her name is Diana. She has frizzy brown hair and laughs even when something isn't funny. Dad and Mom used to hang out with super fit athletes. This woman is so thin, it doesn't look she has any muscles at all. She's like a skeleton with skin. Her eyes dart around a lot and she talks about how to get money, and then laughs. She wondered aloud how much the couch would sell for. I left the room before she assessed my worth. I guess I don't mind Dad dating if he'll stay off drugs, but I don't think this woman is going to help him.

*Sunday, January 9, 1994—12:50 P.M.*

Diana stayed overnight. I know because they made lots of noise until late and I couldn't sleep. The walls of this apartment are thin. There was a lot of panting and grunting and shrieking. I finally put a pillow on my head, hoping to drown them out. They were making the same noises when I woke up, so I stayed in my room until it was quiet. I finally left my room to get some cereal. Both of them were passed out on the sofa—naked. It was gross.

*Wednesday, January 12, 1994—9:10 P.M.*

The principal called me into his office today. My hands were shaking and I felt like I was going to throw up. I wondered if my teacher told him that I don't pay attention and sometimes read library books during class.

I was right. Mr. Flannigan said Miss Michaels is concerned, because I seem like I'm zoned out and not looking at the board. He was impressed that my report cards from my other schools show almost perfect grades, even when I was moving around so much. He asked me what book I'm reading right now. I told him I just finished reading Tom Clancy's latest book.

He looked surprised and said it's not appropriate for a young girl. He suggested I read Judy Blume's books, but I read them already.

He said my test scores from my last school are consistent with an above average 8th grader. What would I think about going to junior high school early?

Since I'm one of the tallest students in the school, he thinks I'd fit in okay. I don't know many people yet, so I'm fine with it.

He's going to discuss this with Dad. He told me that I should pay attention in class, since I'll have to get used to it in junior high.

*Saturday, January 15, 1994—8:15 P.M.*

I want to talk with Dad about going to junior high school, but Diana is here. She's so twitchy. She can't sit still for more than 2 minutes. I went to the kitchen to get some cereal and she stood next to me the entire time. I thought she was going to snatch the box out of my hand.

We're running low on food, and I wanted to eat the rest of the Cheerios before she got her hands on the box. I asked Dad when he was going to the grocery store, but he seemed out of it and didn't respond. I took my bowl into my room and closed the door. My stash of food I collected before coming home is still in the closet. It could last a month if I stretch it.

I'm afraid snoopy Diana will come in here and find it while I'm at school. I wish I had a door lock.

*Monday, January 17, 1994—7:35 P.M.*

Mr. Flannigan called me into his office after school. I'm

going to junior high! I don't know how he got in touch with Dad, but it doesn't matter. I start tomorrow. I'm signed up for English, algebra, and history. The two elective classes I picked are P.E. and home economics. Maybe I can sew some new clothes.

*Friday, January 21, 1994—8:50 P.M.*

It's weird to be starting a new school with older kids. The girls only talk about boys and some of them wear make-up. Two girls were in the bathroom, applying eye shadow and mascara, because their parents don't allow it. I guess they take it off before they go home. There were kids smoking cigarettes in the parking lot and I heard some other kids talking about going to a beer keg.

I tried not to stand out too much. I wore jeans and a top, and focused on my classes. I got free breakfast and lunch, and sat at the end of a table filled with other kids. No one talked to me, but that was okay. I was hungry and wanted to enjoy the food. Dad still hasn't gone grocery shopping.

*Sunday, January 22, 1994—9:10 P.M.*

Dad spent another weekend with Diana, and I stayed in my room. I wanted to go running, swimming, or to the library, but I didn't want to leave my room unlocked. I stayed home and guarded my box of food.

When they were asleep, I cooked some spam and ate it in my room. I put the leftovers in a piece of foil and hid it in the back of the fridge. They must have found it, because it was gone later that day. I haven't asked Dad if he lost his job. If Diana ever leaves, I can find out what's happening.

*Thursday, January 26, 1994—5:45 P.M.*

Schoolwork in junior high isn't as hard as I thought

it would be. As long as I pay attention in class and do homework at night, I'm fine. Time goes by much faster when I'm listening to the teachers and taking notes. There are a few girls I've been talking to at school, but they're older and we don't really have much in common. Even though I'm tall, I think they can tell that I'm younger than them.

The breakfasts and lunches are better than those at elementary school and it's easy to collect some extra food the other kids don't eat off their trays. I usually take home a few apples, oranges, or cookies each day. I brought my food stash to school and put it in my locker. I take home what I need, but I usually eat the food I collected from other students at night, rather than depleting my stash.

## Chapter Thirteen

Kimberly ate the last Oreo. It would have been okay if she'd only eaten the last cookie. But, she'd had the last dozen before Story and Betsy had had a chance to have any.

"You suck!" Story said.

"Hey, I was hungry." Kimberly licked cookie crumbs off her fingers. "Aren't you trying to lose weight?"

Story stuck her tongue out at her sister and marched out of the room. It wasn't a very mature move, but she had a lifetime ahead of her to act responsible and be sophisticated. No need to start early.

She was secretly pleased that the Oreos were gone and wouldn't be a temptation. On the other hand, the pot roast cooking in the oven smelled heavenly. She didn't have to uncover the pots on the stove to know that mashed potatoes and gravy would accompany one of her favorite meals. She wouldn't be surprised if Nina had made a pie or cake for dessert.

She ran up the stairs to her room where library books on the suffrage movement were spread across her bed. She was engrossed in research for another history paper. She'd gotten her first A on her Holocaust term paper. She'd researched the role of train transport to death camps, because she was truly curious about what it had been like. Now, she was exploring how it must have felt for women to be prohibited from voting. Even though she was too young to vote, she reasoned that it wasn't the same, because she knew that when she turned eighteen, she'd have full rights to vote—equal to men.

For the first time ever, Story was learning that she could achieve whatever she wanted if she worked hard enough. It also felt good to activate her brain. She would read, take notes, and contemplate the issues she was reading about. She was also starting to formulate opinions about what she was learning. Once she'd researched the Holocaust, she did additional research about genocide and was surprised to discover that it had occurred in Armenia, Rwanda, Cambodia, and Darfur, too.

"Dinner's ready!" Mom yelled.

"Okay, Mom," Story called back.

By the time she reached the dining room, her parents and sisters were already eating. She sat in her usual chair and filled her plate with her favorite foods. She was right; there was cherry pie for dessert.

"How's school?" Dad asked.

Instead of responding with her usual "fine," Story explained what she was learning about the suffrage movement. Then, she went on to explain her opinions about civil rights. Her parents exchanged looks.

"What?" she asked.

"We're happy you're finally engaged in school," Mom said.

Story suppressed a smile and returned to eating her mashed potatoes. She would wait until later to tell them she was thinking about majoring in history in college.

***

*Sunday, January 29, 1994—7:15 P.M.*

There's absolutely no food in the apartment this weekend and I'm hungry. I only brought a few pieces of fruit and a can of spam home, and by this afternoon, I was so hungry and pissed off that I yelled at Dad. I told him I'd call CPS myself if he wasn't going to feed me or take care of me.

There's no toilet paper, unless I steal some from school or the library. We've run out of soap and toothpaste. Diana hasn't been around for the past few days. Maybe she realized there wasn't any way to make money off of us.

Dad said he was sorry, and finally admitted that he's not working. He lost his job at the car dealership a month ago.

"How are you going to pay rent?" I demanded.

He said he has one more commission check coming, and he's applied for unemployment and food stamps. I demanded that he give me the food stamps so he doesn't trade them for drugs, then I slammed my bedroom door.

*Saturday, May 14, 1994—8:19 P.M.*

It's been months since I've written anything. At first, I was too depressed to write. Dad went downhill again. We were evicted and had to live in a storage shed for a while. I couldn't shower and my clothes were dirty. I was too embarrassed to go to school.

Social Services caught up with us, and I'm back in foster care, attending a different school. I hope the family doesn't read this, because they're super weird. Mrs. Consillio is a chain smoker and spends all her time sitting on the porch, watching the neighbors as if she's watching a soap opera. Then she reports on what everyone's doing at dinner.

There are 4 foster kids here, plus they have 3 of their own kids in a super small house. Us foster kids sleep in a room with bunk beds and the other kids have the other room. There are at least 6 cats and 3 dogs, and the house smells. The cats and dogs poop and pee everywhere, but no one seems to care.

*Tuesday, May 16, 1994—8:30 P.M.*

I sleep on the top bunk. Gina, who is seven years old and hardly ever talks, sleeps below me. Mikey and Davey sleep in the other bunks. They're both in 3rd grade. The Consillios got me so I can take care of the little kids, which means I have to make sure they get up, get dressed, and brush their teeth. I'm also making them keep our room clean and cat and dog free. At least our room doesn't smell too bad.

It has lots of cockroaches, though. They're all over the house, and sometimes, they crawl on us while we sleep. Eww! Gina wants to sleep with me on the top bunk, because she's afraid. I don't like this place.

*Friday, May 19, 1994—9:15 P.M.*

Mrs. Consillio bought me 2 pairs of jeans that are actually long enough, so I don't have to wear high waters. I'm not embarrassed at school now that I look sort of normal. My hair is down to my waist, because I haven't gotten a haircut in ages. I still cut my own bangs, and if I have a sharp enough scissors, they look pretty good.

When Social Services picked me up a few months ago, they took me to a doctor to make sure I was okay. I was examined and given some shots. The doctor said I'm 5 foot, 9 inches tall, which is really tall for an eleven-year-old. He said I need to gain some weight. I guess I weigh 102 pounds, which I think is a lot, but he doesn't.

The kids at school call me "giraffe" or "stilts." I'm used to it. I think I can gain weight at this school, because they feed us pizza, hot dogs, and hamburgers for lunch. We have lots of spaghetti with cut up hot dogs and tomato sauce or hot dogs with buns at the Consillios' house.

## Chapter Fourteen

Every year, all the kids went to see their pediatrician for a check-up. Usually Mom took them together, but this year, she took Story by herself. Now that she was seventeen years old, she noticed her parents were treating her more like an adult.

"I'm not going to be in the room with you," Mom said on the way to the doctor's office.

Story shrugged.

"She's going to examine your private parts and talk to you about birth control."

"Mom!"

"I've talked to you many times about not having sex before you get married," Mom explained. "But, in case you do, I don't want you to get pregnant unexpectedly."

Story rolled her eyes. That was the last thing she was thinking about right now. She'd managed to get Matt off her mind. There were a few boys in her class she had her eye on, but neither of them seemed interested. Jake was a football player who only hung out with guys. She'd never talked to him, but she loved his smile and the way he tossed his blond head back when he laughed. Damon sat next to her in Language Arts. He was tall, had dark brown eyes, and Story thought he might be part Indian. They'd only talked about school so far.

"Are you seeing any boys right now?" Mom interrupted her thoughts.

"Seeing them?"

"You know—dating?"

Story shook her head. "No."

The doctor was a pretty woman with her long dark hair in a ponytail. She asked Story some questions and examined her, just as her mom had warned. She assured her there was no reason to get on birth control.

"Feel free to make an appointment if the need should ever arise," Dr. Barnett said. "I'm concerned about your weight. You're about 15 pounds heavier than you should be."

Story looked down at her bare feet. She'd lost *some* weight, but after she stopped obsessing about Matt, she'd gained it back, along with another 5 pounds.

"Are you involved in any sports?"

"Last year, I swam on the school's swim team," Story said. "But, I quit."

Dr. Barnett nodded. "Why?"

Story shrugged.

"I suggest you become more active. Try eating less sugar and processed foods. I'll talk to your mom about this."

Story hoped she wouldn't have to go on a diet. Maybe she should try jogging or riding a bike. Lately, all she wanted to do was work on homework. She'd managed to bring up her grades to a B average. If she exercised all the time, she doubted she'd be able to get into a good college. But, she'd be thinner…

***

*Wednesday, May 24, 1994—8:35 P.M.*

I've got lots of homework in algebra, biology, and social studies. Most days, I stay after school to finish it, because the Consillios' house is too noisy. Plus, there's no place to sit except on the living room sofa, the floor, or my bunk bed.

Mrs. Consillios doesn't want the kids to sit at the kitchen table or hang out in the kitchen while she's cooking. There's a small TV on the counter and she likes to watch talk shows while preparing dinner. The best thing is that I don't have to help cook. All I have to do is clear the table and put dishes in the dishwasher.

*Sunday, May 28, 1994—5:30 P.M.*

On Friday, I talked to a school counselor, Mrs. McCoy. She wanted to see me, because she said a few of my teachers think I'm depressed. Of course I'm depressed! My life sucks. I live in a small room with 3 little kids I have to take care of. They're not even my brothers or sister. The house is infested with bugs and is filthy. There's cat hair in our food. I don't have any friends at school. My dad is a drug addict and can't take care of me. My mom passed away. I'm all alone and have no idea how long I'll stay at each foster home. Mrs. McCoy covered her mouth with her hands. Her eyes were watering after I told her all this.

I paused for a few minutes to let it all sink in, then I started bawling uncontrollably. I couldn't stop. Finally, Mrs. McCoy left the room and came back with the principal.

They took me in the car to a pediatrician's office. The doctor saw me right away. I curled up in a fetal position on the table and he gave me a shot of something in my arm. In a few minutes, I calmed down and became very tired. I slept all weekend. I have a feeling that I won't be living here much longer.

*Saturday, July 23, 1994—8:52 P.M.*

It's been two months since I've journaled. Where do I start? I'm living at a different place now. With all that's happened in the past few years, I feel numb. The psychologist I've been seeing thinks my depression is *situational*. He thinks that if I get in a good environment, I'll "thrive."

I'm not exactly sure what he means by that, because I don't think I've thrived at any time in my life. I get good grades, because I'd rather read and do homework than deal with the crazy people I've been forced to live with. Everyone thinks I'm 3 years older than my real age, because I'm tall and I have to act grown up to survive. Maybe I'll continue to act older and I'll be able to drive, graduate, get a job, and get an apartment years before I would otherwise. It would be nice not to have to depend on anyone else.

# Chapter Fifteen

Story ironed her black pants and pulled on a red polo shirt, the uniform for her new job. It was the summer before her senior year and there was no way she was going to sit around the house like she'd done last summer. It wasn't hard to convince her parents that she should be allowed to have a summer job. They agreed that she needed to acquire some job skills and suggested she work part-time at a department store at the mall.

Despite their urging, she didn't fill out any applications at the mall. Instead, Story went to every restaurant in town until she was hired by Gino's, an Italian restaurant a few miles away. She'd start out as a hostess and bus person. If she did well, the manager promised she could train as a lunch waitress.

Carmela, a busty dark-haired young woman with a mole near her red lips, showed Story how to greet customers, identify where they should be seated to avoid "slamming" the waiters, and how to lead them to the table. After shadowing Carmela a few times, Story led a couple and their young son to a table and handed them menus. "Your waiter will be right with you," she said.

"Did you ask them if they wanted a booster seat for the little boy?" Carmela asked when she returned to the hostess station.

Story shook her head. It hadn't occurred to her.

Carmela sighed loudly, carried a booster seat to the table, and helped the mother put her son on it.

Next, Story led a family to a four-top table near the other family and handed them their menus.

This time, Carmela complained that Story had seated two tables in Maurice's section too close together in time.

The family should've been put in Tina's section. Story refrained from rolling her eyes. She nodded and smiled. Nothing was going to get in her way of becoming a waitress and earning tips.

Soon, there was a line out the door and Carmela and Story took turns seating the customers. Her co-worker had become too busy to criticize her. When the lunch rush was almost over, a bald man wearing a Gino's polo shirt approached her and introduced himself as Gino. He was the owner and Carmela's father.

"How's she doing?" Story overheard Gino ask his daughter.

"She's coming along," Carmela said.

Story smiled. It wasn't easy work, because she was always moving. But she was burning calories and making money. It sure beat sitting around the house.

When she arrived home that night, Story was exhausted. She changed into her pajamas and curled up with Zana's diary.

*Tuesday, July 26, 1994—7:07 P.M.*

I didn't mention yet where I'm living. The woman's name is Melody Wise and she's the director for the Miss California pageant. She lives in this big house alone (until I showed up), but it seems like there are always people coming and going. The pageant contestants come here for evening gown fittings, talent practice, and all sorts of classes Melody teaches. There are clothes, shoes, and makeup all over the place. All everyone talks about is the pageant.

Melody and a lot of the girls tell me I look like a model and that I should try out for some junior pageant. I did a little modeling when I was younger with my mom. It's okay, but kind of stressful. I like to sew, read, swim, bike, and run. I don't want to walk the runway and have people stare at me.

*Friday, July 29, 1994—8:15 P.M.*

I'm sure many people would be surprised to hear, but this place is my least favorite so far. I don't mind that the place is messy with clothes and makeup and stuff all over the place. There's food to eat and interesting people to talk to.

What I can't stand is Melody. She is critical of every little thing I do. It's like having one of those drill sergeants you see in the movies, standing over me and telling me everything I do is wrong. She criticizes the time I wake up—either too early or too late. My hair needs a hot oil treatment and my bangs are crooked. My clothes don't fit right and are not fashionable. I slouch. I misspeak and my voice is too soft. I eat too much. I don't wear makeup. I'm not helping her enough. Almost everything that comes out of Melody's mouth is a critique.

Since it's summer vacation, I can't escape the house much. I don't know the neighborhood and I'm afraid to ask her to take me swimming or to a library. There are bookshelves with paperback novels in the family room, so I've been reading them when she's not making me help her with the contestants. I can't wait for school to start.

*Wednesday, August 10, 1994—9:15 P.M.*

There hasn't been much to write about until today. We're getting ready for a pageant. I haven't paid much attention to the details, because I'm not all that interested in plastic smiles and bikini poses.

One of the girls, Desiree, needed someone to alter her dress for the opening dance number. I volunteered, because I don't get many opportunities to use Melody's sewing machine. After Melody left with the other girls, Desiree and I worked on her dress.

I worked fast, because it had to be done before Melody returned. When we were finished, Desiree asked me why I was living there. I told her that I'm a foster child.

It turns out that she was, too. She just aged out of the system and is competing in pageants to win scholarship money for college. Desiree's father committed suicide and her mother is in jail. She's been on her own for a few years.

We traded stories about our foster home experiences. Desiree said that she finally got sick of it and ended up on the street. She didn't want to tell me at first, but then she said it would be good for me to know so it won't happen to me, too. She was a teenage prostitute for about seven months and then got arrested. Melody stepped in as a foster parent and turned Desiree's life around. That's how she ended up competing in pageants.

When Melody returned, I felt some respect for her and wasn't as annoyed when she complained about the messy sewing room.

*Saturday, August 13, 1994—10:35 P.M.*

Today was a weird day. Melody helped out at a fashion show and she made me go, too. She doesn't like me to stay alone all day in her house and "get into things."

I brought a book to read, but Melody volunteered me to help with final fittings. One of the designer's dresses didn't fit the model. The designer suggested that I try it on.

It fit perfectly and I got to be in the fashion show! My hair was styled, and they put makeup on my face (first time), and I walked down the runway wearing a short, form-fitting white dress.

The photographer took a few Polaroid pictures and gave them to me "for my portfolio." When the hairdresser worked on my hair, he cut my bangs straight and showed me how to cut them correctly. I think he might have guessed I'm a foster child. The makeup made my eyes look amazing. I wish I could wear it all the time, but the makeup artist, Pandi, said I'm too young.

Melody showed me how to walk down the runway in heels. We practiced quite a bit until I was not so wobbly. I was worried I'd fall, but one of the models told me to focus on the beat of the music and relax.

I managed to walk without falling and Melody even gave me a compliment. "Good job, Zana," she said. I'll take it.

*Wednesday, August 17, 1994—8:50 P.M.*

This summer, I've read 42 books so far. There's not much else to do. Finally, Melody came into my room on Monday and asked me why all I do is read.

I shrugged my shoulders. If I didn't say anything, she might not criticize me.

She said, "School starts soon. Is there anything you'd like to do?"

I said, "Swim."

"Why didn't you say something earlier, Zana?"

Again, I shrugged my shoulders.

She dropped me off at her country club swimming pool yesterday and today. It's beautiful. I swam laps for an hour each day and couldn't stop smiling. Melody seemed pleased with herself that she'd solved the glum Zana problem.

## Chapter Sixteen

Today was Story's first day off from Gino's in ten days. She'd filled in for anyone who asked her to take a shift. By now, she felt comfortable as hostess and bus person. Soon she'd tell the manager she felt ready to try waitressing.

"What do you want to do today?" Mom asked.

"I was thinking about going swimming, but Erica and Whitney both have to work," Story said. She hadn't been swimming since January, and as the weather grew warmer, she longed to cool off in the water.

Mom gave her a sideways glance. "Why don't you take your sisters?"

"You mean *drive* them in my car?" Story wasn't sure she understood her mother. She'd never been allowed to drive anyone but her parents.

"Sure," Mom said. "Be careful."

The country club pool was crowded. Kimberly and Betsy dove into the water immediately. Story set up her towel on a lounge chair, cracked open the can of soda she'd brought, and opened her novel to the first page.

"Hey, there," an unfamiliar male voice said.

She looked up. There was Jake standing over her, wearing red shorts and a white tank top. She guessed he had a job as a lifeguard.

She smiled, sat up straighter, and sucked in her stomach. "Hi."

"I recognize you from school. Aren't you Story Sanchez?"

She nodded. She tried to think of something to say but felt tongue-tied.

"I'm Jake Keller." He grinned. "You were in my homeroom and algebra classes last year."

"Oh, yeah." She couldn't believe he actually *knew* who

she was. Jake was the most popular guy in school.

"I have to get to my station. If it's okay, I'll come back and talk to you during my next break."

"Sure," she said. "That would be great." She smiled at him. She was relieved she had on sunglasses that hid the excitement in her eyes.

After he returned to the lifeguard stand, she ducked into the bathroom and looked in the mirror. She was wearing the orange bikini she'd bought with her first paycheck. Even though she'd been eating pizza at the restaurant, she looked trimmer than she had in months—probably from being on her feet most days. If she sucked in her stomach, she looked good.

She'd worn her waist-long hair loose and it hung down over her shoulders. Thankfully, she was able to avoid her friends' anxiety about getting a tan, because her skin was naturally olive.

When she returned to her lounge chair, Kimberly had pulled a chair up next to hers. Her sister was only twenty months younger. Some said they looked like twins, except Kimberly was an inch shorter, wore a bigger bra size, and was far more outgoing than Story was.

"I saw that cute lifeguard talking to you," Kimberly said.

"Shhh! Not so loud," Story said. "He's a classmate."

"If you're not going to date him, introduce him to me. He's hot!"

Story shook her head. "He's mine." She had to call dibs, otherwise Kimberly would flirt with him.

That was something Story wasn't as good at, either. Ever since they were in elementary school, Kimberly seemed to be better at everything than her older sister. She got better grades, she excelled at whatever sport she tried out for, and she was more popular with the other kids.

Kimberly stuck out her lip in a pout.

"Don't you have a boyfriend?" Story asked.

"I can shop around a little, can't I?"

Story shook her head. Kimberly had been dating Mark Fitzgerald, a boy she'd met on the track team. As far as Story knew, they were still together. It was probably Kimberly's behavior that had planted the idea of birth control in Mom's head.

"There are two of you!" Jake said as he approached, carrying two plastic cups of iced soda. He handed it to Story and then pulled up a chair next to her.

"Thank you. Jake, this is my sister, Kimberly. She was just going back into the pool with our other sister, weren't you?" Story glared at her sister over her sunglasses.

Kimberly smiled and said hi to Jake and then rolled her eyes at Story. She did as her sister asked and headed back to the pool.

"I know what it's like. I have a younger brother." Jake leaned back in his chair and sipped his drink. "I haven't seen you here before."

"I know. I've been busy working at Gino's during the day." But now she wished she'd taken the summer off to hang out at the pool.

"They have great pizza." Jake paused. "What time do you get off? Maybe I can stop by sometime."

Story felt her stomach stir. "Usually about three."

"Okay, then. What if—" Jake was interrupted by the other lifeguard who was calling his name.

Jake jumped up and raced over to the side of the pool where a crowd was beginning to gather.

Someone yelled, "Call nine-one-one!"

Story couldn't see what had happened, but within minutes, everyone was ordered out of the pool and asked to leave. As they walked out of the gate, paramedics and police officers ran in. She lingered around the entryway with a half dozen others, all conjecturing what had caused the commotion. Someone said that a little boy had been pulled out of the water. Story hoped that he was okay.

***

*Friday, August 19, 1994—9:15 P.M.*

Melody gave me a stack of five different fabrics I can use to sew school clothes. She told me to help myself to the box of notions—zippers, buttons, etc. There's also a big box of patterns for me to use. I plan on sewing every minute I'm not at the pool until school starts.

Today, I made a floral top, and tomorrow I'm going to

attempt some pants. I think Melody suggested I sew to keep me busy while she does promotional work for an upcoming pageant. She's been leaving me home alone all week. I heard her tell someone on the phone that if I'm focused on sewing, I don't have time to get into trouble.

*Friday, August 26, 1994—8:33 P.M.*

It's nice to be in school and get out of the house. But that's about the only positive thing I have to say.

Again, I don't know a soul. I wish I were bubbly and outgoing. I've heard people call me stuck up behind my back at other schools, and I've never been able to understand why they have that impression. I'm shy. Even if someone starts the conversation, I don't know what to say.

Today, a girl named Savannah sat next to me in math and started babbling about her classes and something about going to the lake for summer vacation.

I smiled and listened, because I didn't know what else to do. I told her my name and that I think school should start after Labor Day.

She invited me to sit with her at lunch, so I sat with her and her pretty friends. I smiled and listened.

They asked me what I did over the summer and I said I read, sewed clothes, and modeled in a fashion show. I'm surprised at how much that modeling experience impressed them.

*Tuesday, August 30, 1994—7:42 P.M.*

It turns out that the girls I've been eating lunch with are the "popular" girls. I asked another girl, Kerry, about the book she was reading in the library, and we ended up talking for a while about books.

Kerry is the only interesting person I've met in a long time. She reads a lot and can talk about all sorts of books and topics. I asked her about eating lunch together and she laughed. She said that popular girls don't hang out with nerds.

“What are you talking about?” I asked.

“You sit with the popular girls,” she said, and then walked away.

I spent lunchtime listening to Savannah and her friends talk about Jennifer Aniston’s new haircut and the movie *Dumb and Dumber*. I smiled and pretended to be interested.

*Friday, September 23, 1994—9:35 P.M.*

I’ve been so busy with school. I like my social studies class. We’re studying famous lawyers throughout history, like Woodrow Wilson, Cicero, William Howard Taft, Thomas Cromwell, John Marshall, Thurgood Marshall, John Jay, Earl Warren, John Foster Dulles, Clarence Darrow, and Abraham Lincoln. I raised my hand and asked if there were any famous women lawyers, and everyone laughed at me. I thought that since our First Lady, Hillary Rodham Clinton, was also a lawyer, she should at least be mentioned. When I raised this, the other kids laughed at me.

*Sunday, September 25, 1994—8:55 P.M.*

It looks like I’ll be moving again. I was so busy with school that I hadn’t noticed that Melody hasn’t been around much. I didn’t think to ask her if anything was wrong. I usually stay away from her if I can avoid it, because the only things she usually says are criticisms or orders me to do something. She hasn’t asked me once about school, so I assumed that she wasn’t interested.

She asked me to sit down at the kitchen table to discuss something important. At first, I thought she was going to tell me I need to vacuum better or clean the windows. Instead, she told me that she has breast cancer. She got the diagnosis a few weeks ago and will be starting chemotherapy in a few days. I need to pack my things, because she can’t continue to foster me.

I’ll be leaving the day after tomorrow. I didn’t know

what to say and was silent for a few minutes.

I finally said, "I'm so sorry," hugged her, and thanked her for everything. I hope she doesn't die like my mother did.

*Monday, September 26, 1994—9:20 P.M.*

I'm all packed and ready to go. I'm not sorry to leave this house. I've never felt comfortable here. I'm not sorry to leave the school. The girls act fake and boring.

I have a stomachache. I think it's because I'm scared my new foster home will be even worse.

*Wednesday, September 28, 1994—9:15 P.M.*

At first, I was sort of relieved and happy when Dad picked me up. I thought maybe things would be different this time.

He says they are. He's got a job at a coffee shop in Newport Beach. It turns out that he borrowed the car he was driving from a friend and that he only has a studio apartment.

I have to sleep on a twin mattress on the floor in the corner. He gave me about 5 inches of closet space to hang up clothes and 2 drawers in an old dresser.

After I emptied my Hefty bags of clothes, he wanted me to unpack my box. I said I'd do it later. It's my box of food I've been stockpiling in case I ended up at Dad's or someplace else with no food.

Knowing Dad, he'll rummage through it when he's looking for something valuable to sell for drugs. I've got to figure out how to hide it.

I asked him why I wasn't sent to live with another family. He said CPS tracked him down. There aren't any foster homes available, so they told him to pick me up.

This totally sucks! No wonder he's not ready for me to move in.

*Thursday, September 29, 1994—6:15 P.M.*

I talked Dad into letting me start school on Monday, instead of mid-week. He's working right now, allowing me time to clean the floors, the kitchen, and bathroom. It's disgusting! I don't think Dad has ever cleaned the toilet, shower, or floors.

He must have gone grocery shopping before picking me up, because there's cereal, milk, bread, peanut butter, and some frozen dinners—more food than usual.

I looked through his drawers and found drug paraphernalia and a baggie of marijuana. I want to flush it down the toilet, but I'm too afraid. I found something hidden under his mattress that's even more scary.

*Sunday, October 2, 1994—8:05 P.M.*

Dad totally bamboozled me. This isn't his apartment. It's his girlfriend Renee's ex-husband's place. She's pissed about me living here. They've been yelling at each other all weekend.

Renee said, "She can't be here" and, "the little bitch has to go," right in front of me.

It's not like I have anywhere else to go. I sit on my mattress and read the only book I have—John Grisham's *The Client* over and over again.

Dad tried to stick up for me, but she was adamant that the condominium rules only allow two people to live in a studio and she didn't want her ex—Ralph—to get into trouble.

I'm afraid to do anything more than use the bathroom and I wait until I almost burst before I do that.

When Dad went out for a smoke (I guess he smokes cigarettes now) and Renee was using the bathroom, I quickly ate a granola bar from my box and hid the wrapper in my suitcase. I don't know if I'm going to school tomorrow. I don't want to leave my stuff. She might throw it into a dumpster and lock me out.

*Friday, October 7, 1994—9:10 P.M.*

After a week of craziness, Dad took me to CPS's office today. I didn't go to school this week. I just sat on that thin twin mattress and snuck food from my box whenever I could. Dad gave me a hot dog or cereal now and then, but I felt like an unwanted stray dog. I still do.

I'm staying at a homeless shelter for the weekend, because CPS doesn't have a place for me. There are lots of rules and I'm scared. I don't think I'll be able to sleep tonight. The lady sleeping in the bunk above me is making weird noises. It smells like corn chips and urine.

I've eaten all the food I have with me that isn't in cans. I didn't go to dinner, because I'm afraid someone will steal my stuff.

I am relieved to be out of Renee's place. I worried she might use the gun I found under her mattress on Dad or I. I wanted to tell Dad about it, but I only got about a minute alone with him before they dropped me off.

Story put Zana's diary back in its hiding place, crawled back into bed, and pulled Maggie close to her. It was hard to believe all these things had happened to a real girl. She'd seen a few Lifetime television shows about girls who were in foster homes until a family adopted them, but she'd never heard of someone struggle like Zana. She wondered where the diary's author was now. Was there some way to help her?

Story fell asleep thinking about Zana, then dreamt that she was trapped in an elevator with Maggie. There was no food or water, and she screamed to get out. She woke up in a sweat with her mother leaning over her.

"Are you okay?" she asked.

Story stared wide-eyed at her mother.

"It was only a bad dream." Mom smoothed her hair and kissed her on the forehead. "I'll be right here. Now, go back to sleep."

Story reached out and squeezed Mom's hand before she closed her eyes.

She couldn't shake the nightmare she'd had last night as she worked the evening shift at Gino's. She showed one group after the other to their tables, presented them with menus, and told them that their waiter would be with them shortly. Ordinarily, she'd make the extra effort to assist with waters, clear plates, or expedite food, but tonight, her mind was elsewhere.

During a lull in business, she leaned against the hostess podium and stared into space until Frank, the owner, asked her to check on table fourteen. Story gave him a broad smile and replied, "Absolutely," and did as he asked. The one thing that Zana had taught her was to appreciate the opportunities she had.

***

*Wednesday, November 9, 1994—8:35 P.M.*

When I'm super depressed, it's hard for me to do anything. That's why I haven't been writing. I guess things are getting a little better.

It took me a week before I moved out of the shelter, but during that week, Dad came by almost every day. His eyes were wild, he smelled, and he slurred his speech. I don't know where he expected me to go with him. Renee kicked him out.

Finally, I got placed with a family back in Ventura. They seem kind of normal. I live with Mr. and Mrs. Abbott, their sons Ted and Todd, and their daughter, Jami.

They haven't had a foster kid for a few years, but the agency talked them into taking me, since there was nowhere else for me to go.

They seem like a tight-knit family—Ted is eighteen years old and works construction. Todd is fifteen and seems shy. Jami is a twelve-year-old tomboy and soccer player.

Funny thing is, Todd seems more feminine that Jami. He dresses in pink t-shirts and Jami has short hair and looks like a boy. I thought they were all boys at first.

I have my own room in the basement, which is a little scary, but also cool. My bedroom is pretty basic—a twin bed, small dresser, and a small closet with a gray carpeted floor. Next to it, there's a bathroom with a toilet and sink.

Their cats' litter box and shelves for storage are in an adjacent downstairs room. They have two cats.

I have to go upstairs to the main floor to shower in the bathroom the kids all share. The kids' bedrooms, kitchen, dining room, and living room are also on the main floor. Mr. and Mrs. Abbott's master bedroom and an office are on the top floor. Mrs. Abbott said she's a realtor and her husband is a manager at a factory. Guess I'll learn soon what interesting quirks they have.

*Monday, November 14, 1994—9:20 P.M.*

There hasn't been much drama in this house or at my new school. The Abbotts eat dinner together. Mr. Abbott and Ted do all the talking. The others just eat their food and listen. So far, they've been too busy talking about football to talk to me much. I'm fine with it, because I'm enjoying every bite of roast chicken, meatloaf, spaghetti, and tacos that Mrs. Abbott makes. We even had chocolate cake for dessert tonight, and it wasn't a special occasion.

I haven't made any friends at school, but I'm okay with it. Mrs. Abbott bought me a few sweaters—one is black and the other is brown. I think the sweaters are like camouflage, because no one seems to notice me.

*Friday, November 18, 1994—7:48 P.M.*

It's been a long time since my life seemed like it was on a schedule like it is now. I get up at 6:30 A.M., get ready, and eat cereal and a banana for breakfast. I catch a school bus at 7:30. I have classes until 3 P.M., then I go to swim practice. I take the late bus, which drops me off about 5 blocks away, and I walk to the Abbotts' place from there. I do about an hour of homework, we have dinner, and then I go to my room to do more homework. I sit on my bed, because I don't have a desk. I'm fine with it. I've had much worse.

The family watches TV after dinner every night in the living room. I don't want to intrude, so I tell them

I'm going to do homework and go to bed early. I've been staying up late to read library books after I get my homework done. Having a room in the basement gives me privacy to do what I want. I don't even have to use the kid's bathroom upstairs, because during the week I take a shower after swim practice.

*Tuesday, November 22, 1994*

Even though I haven't made friends at school yet, I sort of wish we didn't have Thanksgiving vacation. I would rather not help cook and clean or have dinner with the Abbotts' relatives, who I don't know.

Last night, Mrs. Abbott asked if I'd like to see Dad for Thanksgiving. I shook my head. I'm looking forward to eating turkey, mashed potatoes, stuffing, and pumpkin pie with whipped cream.

If I managed to see Dad, the only way we'd get food is if we went to some place giving dinners to the homeless. No thank you. I'm going to enjoy every bite of Mrs. Abbott's home-cooked meal. The small talk with strangers will be worth it.

*Friday, November 25, 1994—9:05 P.M.*

It's been nice to have a few days off from school. I spent most of yesterday in the kitchen. I helped make the turkey, stuffing, and most of the side dishes. Guests brought pies and wine.

Once we were finished cooking, I set the table and cleaned the kitchen. When everyone had arrived, I busied myself with making sure they had something to drink. Then I put all the food out with serving spoons. I focused on getting everything done and tried not to talk much.

A few of the Abbotts' relatives asked me questions, but mostly they left me alone. The food was delicious. I ate pumpkin and apple pie for dessert. After dinner, I washed the dishes.

Mr. and Mrs. Abbott thanked me many times for

working so hard. Mrs. Abbott said that for the first time in years, she was able to talk to her relatives and enjoy herself, rather than being a slave in the kitchen. I guess foster kids are good for something.

*Saturday, November 26, 1994—2:10 P.M.*

I had a turkey sandwich and a piece of pumpkin pie for lunch. I'm stuffed. It was almost as good as it was on Thanksgiving. I depleted my entire box of emergency food before coming here, so I'm starting it again. The pantry is so full, I'm sure Mrs. Abbott won't miss the cans of beans or the box of macaroni and cheese I took. This time, I'm also going to stock toilet paper, soap, and some other necessities. Even though things seem to be going well with this family, I have to be prepared they might kick me out any day.

*Sunday, November 27, 1994—8:45 P.M.*

I'm glad I have school tomorrow. I'm sick of sitting in my room and reading. I helped Mrs. Abbott clean the house today, and yesterday, I helped Mr. Abbott with some yard work. Other than that, all I've done is finish my homework and read. I hope I make some friends soon. I'm lonely.

# Chapter Seventeen

Anthony and Brooke came home for Thanksgiving. Story got all her homework done ahead of time and temporarily moved back into Kimberly's room. Brooke shared with Betsy, and Anthony slept in his old room. Story wondered if Brooke would try to sneak into Anthony's room during the night when everyone was asleep. Her parents still didn't know that they were living together.

When she and Anthony were alone in the kitchen while the others were playing a game of Monopoly in the living room, Story asked, "How are things going?"

"Good. We're both busy with work and school."

"I meant, silly, how is it living with her?"

"We've had some challenges." He paused and looked down at his shoes.

"You can tell me." Story put her hand on his shoulder, something she'd never done before.

"She had a miscarriage." His voice quavered.

"Oh, that's horrible. I'm sorry." Story didn't know what else to say. "How far along was she?"

"Two months. We were planning on going to the courthouse to get married in a few weeks, and then she lost the baby." Tears welled in Anthony's eyes.

"How long ago was that?"

"Right before Halloween."

Story reached out and gave Anthony a hug. "What are you going to do now?"

He shook his head. "I have no idea. Brooke doesn't want to talk about it."

"Brooke doesn't want to talk about what?" Mom said as she walked into the room. She opened the fridge and grabbed some cans of soda.

"Nothing," Anthony said.

Mom gave him a concerned look and paused, balancing four cans of soda in her hands.

"Grad school," he blurted.

"Okay," she said. "I thought you were going to say something about your relationship, like marriage. She's a nice girl. If you two want to get married, it's fine with me."

"Thanks, Mom," Anthony said.

After she left the room, Anthony changed the subject to what was going on in Story's life. She told him about waitressing over the summer and how much she liked working and making her own money. She was doing much better in school and had joined the swim team again. She didn't mention that she and Matt were now friends. She couldn't remember what she had seen in him.

"Do you have a boyfriend?" Anthony teased her.

She shook her head. She didn't tell him that she'd hoped to go out with Jake, but a little kid had drowned that day at the pool. She wanted to talk to him about it, but there never seemed to be an opportunity.

During the summer, whenever she went to the pool, he wasn't there. After school started, she didn't talk to him, because he was always surrounded by other football players. She hoped Jake didn't blame her for what had happened.

***

*Tuesday, November 29, 1994—9:20 P.M.*

I'm so embarrassed!!! I was taking a shower in the upstairs bathroom. The door was closed. There's no lock on it, but if no one's in the bathroom, we leave the door open. There hasn't been any problem before. Jami and Todd usually shower in the morning and Ted showers at night. If I have swim practice, I don't use the shower.

There's no swim practice this week, so I took a shower while the family was watching TV. As I stepped out of the shower and was reaching for a towel, Ted walked in. I was completely naked! He just stood there and stared at me.

I quickly grabbed a towel and wrapped myself in it before he left. I almost screamed, but I didn't want everyone to come running into the bathroom while I was naked to see what was wrong.

Ted is a strange guy. He's big and muscular, and even though he's only eighteen, he has a receding hairline. He has a tattoo of a naked woman on his arm! I didn't see it until a week ago when he was wearing a tank top. I wonder if he got in trouble from his parents when he got it.

*Friday, December 2, 1994—8:05 P.M.*

Ted has been following me around the house. It's sort of creepy—like he's stalking me. He's usually really talkative to his family, but he doesn't say much to me. He just stares. I wonder if his parents have noticed. They're polite to me, but I don't feel like part of the family. At least they're nice. They don't make me do many chores, feed me well, and let me have my privacy in my own room. I feel sort of like a pet they keep in the basement.

*Tuesday, December 6, 1994—9:10 P.M.*

I finally made a friend at school. Her name is Victoria, and she doesn't like it when people call her Vicki, Vic, or Tori. She has a beagle named Happy, she likes to ride her bike, and she has green eyes like me. She noticed my eyes and made a comment that she hadn't seen any girls her age with the same color eyes.

I told her that I hadn't, either. She sat with me at lunch, and we tried to figure out if we had any other things in common. Only biking and eye color. She's short, has red hair, and lots of freckles on her face. She has a big Irish family and her dad is a dentist. She and her two sisters have braces on their teeth.

She said she wished they had room for friends to stay overnight at her house, but with 6 kids and only 4 bedrooms, her parents don't allow sleepovers. Her mom says she has too much to do as it is and can't have each of her kids bringing friends over. I wouldn't dare ask the Abbotts if I could invite a friend over.

*Friday, December 9, 1994—8:52 P.M.*

I've been eating lunch with Victoria and her friends, Misty and Jessica. They're really nice. The three of them have known each other since first grade and live on the same block. I don't think they usually let other girls into their tight circle, but they were intrigued that Victoria and I have the same unique eye color. They've been nice. I heard Misty mention going to see the movie *Junior* on Saturday. I don't have any money for a movie, but they didn't invite me anyway.

*Tuesday, December 13, 1994—9:10 P.M.*

It was Victoria's birthday today. Misty brought cupcakes and candles, and a bunch of kids sang the "happy birthday" song at lunch. Victoria just turned 14. I wonder if she knows that I'm 3 years younger.

Since I've been living here, I've tried to dress like the other kids in order to fit in. Mrs. Abbott took me school clothes shopping when I first moved in. I was able to buy some jeans and tops that make me look older. I bought a bra, even though there's nothing to put in it yet. At least my bra straps peek out now and then, so I look less like a kid and hopefully, pass as a teenager. I've never told anyone here that I skipped a few grades and am so much younger than they are. As one of the tallest girls, I constantly fool people about my age. I've notice that if I act confident and smart, no one questions it.

***

Still not allowed to drive any friends in her car, Story met up with Whitney and Erica at the football game. They wore the school colors of burgundy and gold, and rooted for their school's undefeated team.

Story's focus was mostly on Jake, the starting quarterback. Her friends thought he was cute, but they had their eyes on other players. All their friends thought it was cute that Erica was going to the winter dance with the running back, Eric Edwards. They were *the* Eric and Erica, even though they'd only gone on a few dates.

Whitney and tight end, Steve Reynolds, had been friends since junior high and were now flirting with each other. If he didn't ask her to the dance, she planned to ask him.

"What about you, Story? Who are you going with?" Whitney prodded.

Story shrugged her shoulders and turned her attention to number eight on the field. She could see a tuft of his blonde hair peeking out from the back of his helmet. It was long enough to just barely put in a ponytail. She'd never seen Jake wear it that way. She noticed him every day at school. He wore either a surfer t-shirt or a football jersey.

The team won again, and Story jumped up and down with her friends. Then, she watched Jake's teammates drench him and the coach with Gatorade.

Story wondered what would have happened if that little boy hadn't drowned that day at the pool. Would Jake have come by the restaurant to see her? She'd never know.

***

*Friday, December 16, 1994—10:18 P.M.*

We're on winter break now. I'm not sure what to do without homework and school to keep me busy. Victoria, Misty, and Jessica live a few miles away and they didn't mention anything about getting together over break. I heard them talking about some of the things they plan to do, like ice skating, baking Christmas cookies, and having a secret Santa gift exchange. They didn't include me in their discussions, though. I think I'm the girl they eat lunch with. I'm not really part of their group.

*Tuesday, December 20, 1994—9:45 P.M.*

The Abbotts have been super busy since school got out. They're going to Christmas parties and concerts, shopping and baking cookies, and wrapping presents at home. I offer to help, but unless it's with something to do in the kitchen, they usually decline.

On Sunday, we baked 8 dozen cookies. I mixed the dough, shaped the cookies on pans, and timed the baking. I monitored the cooling and placed them in boxes to give away as presents to neighbors and friends.

At first, Jami and Todd hung around, but when they realized I was willing to do the work, they went off to play video games or talk on the phone. I cleaned up the kitchen alone.

*Friday, December 23, 1994—8:35 P.M.*

I had hoped the Abbotts would invite me to some activities, but I haven't been included. Instead, I put the artificial tree up and decorated it with boxes of ornaments. I found more boxes of decorations in the basement and used them to make the rest of the house look festive. I even put some green and red lights on the outside windows and arranged some reindeer, a Santa, and sleigh in the yard.

Mrs. Abbott thanked me, then excused herself to her room to wrap presents.

I checked out some Christmas-themed books from the library so when I don't have anything to do, I can read in my room.

Earlier in the evening, Ted walked into my room without knocking. He stood at the door and didn't say anything. I asked him if I could help him with something. He turned around and left. Weird guy.

*Saturday, December 24, 1994—10:30 P.M.*

We had prime rib for dinner with horseradish sauce. I didn't know what it was and asked Mr. Abbott to pass the pot roast. He laughed, then explained what we were eating. My parents seldom cooked anything fancy, and we'd never had the money for expensive meat. When I was younger, I'd be thrilled to have meatloaf or hamburgers.

There were three different kinds of vegetables, mashed potatoes and gravy, and rolls so flaky they seemed to melt in my mouth. I ate a large piece of apple pie and two Christmas cookies.

Now, I'm lying on my bed, feeling sick to my stomach. I've never eaten so much delicious food in one sitting before.

Mrs. Abbott smiled at me and kept telling me to eat slower—the food wouldn't disappear. Little does she know.

*Sunday, December 25, 1994—8:05 P.M.*

I slept in, because it was the weekend. Jami knocked on my door and said to get up. Her mother must have told her to come downstairs, because I've never seen her or Todd or their parents downstairs. The only one who ever comes down is Ted.

Jami said they were opening presents and I should come up. I have no money, so I didn't buy anyone anything, and certainly didn't expect anything from them.

I put my jeans and a sweater on and joined them around the tree. I was the only one not wearing pajamas. Mr. and Mrs. Abbott wore robes and slippers over their pajamas and sipped coffee. Todd and Jami and even Ted were sitting on the floor, opening piles of gifts. Ripped paper and discarded bows were everywhere.

I sat on the end of the couch and watched until Mrs. Abbott handed me a large box, wrapped in shiny silver and red paper. It seemed like years since I'd received a Christmas present. I just stared at the box until she told me to open it. I didn't want to spoil the beautiful wrapping.

I slowly undid the tape, careful not to tear the paper. The box was filled with brand new clothes—pants, tops, a sweater, a dress, and a Speedo swimsuit. I stared in disbelief. Tears welled up in my eyes. I started crying before I managed to say thank you.

Everyone stopped what they were doing and stared at

me. I don't think they realized how happy I was for their generosity, even though I know that the money for the gift came from the State of California.

# Chapter Eighteen

A few days after Christmas, Story was heading out the door to meet up with her friends to go ice skating for the first time in years. She was wearing the blue sweater and black jeans she'd gotten from Santa for Christmas. Her stomach fluttered with nerves. She wasn't sure if she remembered how to skate and didn't want to make a fool of herself in front of her classmates. When she'd asked who would be there, Erica had said, "Everyone." She knew what that meant.

The rink was packed with football players, cheerleaders, and every cool kid she knew who hadn't gone to Tahoe, Snowbird, or Aspen to ski or snowboard over the holiday. She didn't see Jake, and wondered if he was away with his family for vacation.

It was just as well—the moment she stepped onto the ice she fell on her butt. She would have been horrified if Jake had seen her. One of the boys on the football team, Kevin Bailey, helped her up. He then held her hand until she got used to the ice. Before long, she was skating fast in time with the blaring music around the rink with Erica and Whitney.

They stopped for a hot chocolate break and to rest when a song none of them liked began playing.

"What about Kevin?" Whitney asked.

"What about him?" Story said.

"I think he likes you," Erica said.

Story shrugged. She'd never talked to him before. He was one of the cutest guys in their class, with straight black hair and brown eyes. He dressed as if he was a fashion model and sometimes wore a fedora hat.

"Maybe he'll ask you to the winter dance," Whitney said.

Story didn't respond. The idea of Kevin Bailey asking her to a dance was ludicrous. She'd talked to him one time and he was completely out of her league. The only girls she'd seen with him looked like supermodels compared to her.

They skated until the lights flashed, signaling that the rink would close in fifteen minutes.

After they'd returned their rental skates and collected their shoes, Story felt a tap on her shoulder.

"Hey, beautiful," Kevin said.

At first, Story didn't think he was talking to her. Then she recovered, and said, "Hey."

"Do you want to get something to eat?" he asked.

"I'm with my friends," Story said.

"That's okay, we don't mind," Erica interjected.

"I can take you home later," Kevin said.

It was settled. Story followed Kevin to his BMW and he took her to Kenny's, a twenty-four-hour restaurant that was a popular hang-out near their high school. Before they went in, Kevin pulled out a flask and poured some clear liquid into a partially full soda bottle. They took turns taking sips and talking about school until the bottle was empty. Story was feeling relaxed and a bit unsteady on her feet.

The restaurant was packed with many of the kids who'd been at the rink. Rather than join any of his friends, Kevin led her to a booth and motioned her to sit on the same side as him. They ordered hamburgers and Cokes, and as soon as the waitress left to put in their order, Kevin pulled her in close and kissed her, pressing his tongue inside her mouth.

Her senses dulled by alcohol, Story leaned into him and kissed him back. Soon, their hands were groping each other under the table while they explored each other's mouths with their tongues.

They took a break to eat part of their burgers. Kevin asked for the check, which he immediately paid for with a credit card he handed to the waitress.

"Let's go." He led her by the hand past their classmates back to his BMW. He silently drove to the end of a deserted road and produced another flask and bottle. They drank and made out until Story realized that he didn't intend to stop with just kissing. She moved away from him and pulled down her sweater.

"I need to go home," she said.

"Come on, we're just getting started."

"Please, take me home." Her heart was racing. She wondered what she'd do if he refused.

After pleading with him for a few more minutes, he started the car. They drove in silence to her house. He didn't walk her to the door or kiss her goodnight.

She gave him a half-wave and walked as quietly as she could to the front door. The house was silent. She was relieved her parents weren't awake to see her disheveled hair, smell alcohol on her breath, or see the beard burn on her face.

***

*Thursday, December 29, 1994—9:15 P.M.*

Mrs. Abbott gave me a letter from Dad.

He wrote:

*Dear Z-Bear,*

*I miss you so much. I wish we could have been together for Christmas. I'm back in Ventura, working at a convenience store. Just in case you want to see me, I'm at the 7-11 where we used to go to pick up Gatorade after running. I'm sure you remember it.*

*I'm not going to go on and on, because I don't think you'll get this letter. I've been writing to you every week we've been away from each other, but never get a response. My wish is that someday you'll stop by the store and I can see you.*

*I love you, sweet Z.*

*Always,*

*Dad*

After I read this, I curled up in a ball under my covers and cried until there were no tears left. I missed him, too, and couldn't understand why no one had given me his letters before now. The 7-11 he's working at is about 9 miles away from here.

He didn't put a return address on his letter, so I don't know why he thinks I might write back. He also knows that I'm probably not going to be able to get a ride to a distant 7-11 to see my drug addict, irresponsible father.

The letter was written on the back of a store order form, so I'm sure he's spending his wages on something other than greeting cards.

After I cried it out, I gave the situation some serious thought. Most likely, Dad's managed to keep a job for a month or two, is using drugs as soon as he gets off work, and is living with others or in a horrid rented room or studio. As much as we miss each other, there's no way I can survive living with him. I don't think I'm going to be able to sleep tonight, but I'm glad to hear he's still alive.

*Saturday, December 31, 1994—8:20 P.M.*

Tomorrow is 1995—a new year. As long as I'm living with foster families, I will always be on edge. I don't belong. Even the best families, like the Abbotts, can't do much more than provide me food and shelter. I appreciate this, because even when I was with my dad, he couldn't provide food and barely could provide shelter. He didn't do much in the love department, but I always felt that I belonged.

I want 1995 to be an amazing year, but I don't know how to make that happen. If I find a way to fill my year with what makes me happiest, then maybe it won't matter that I don't belong. The things that make me happy:

1. Swimming
2. Biking
3. Running
4. Competing in triathlons

5. Reading
6. Sewing
7. Getting good grades in school
8. Eating delicious food
9. Having close friends
10. Being with Dad when he's not on drugs

I'm not sure how I can make 2 or 4 happen, since I don't have a bike and have no money for triathlon entry fees. Without a sewing machine and fabric, 6 isn't possible. I have no control over 10. And so, I'll focus on numbers 1, 3, 5, 7, 8 and 9.

Right now, I'm going to go upstairs to the kitchen and eat a slice of chocolate cake (number 8) that Mrs. Abbott left for us. Mr. and Mrs. Abbott are out for the evening. I hear the TV on in the living room. I can eat my cake with the other kids while watching a New Year's Eve special.

*Monday, January 1, 1995, 11:30 A.M.*

Something happened last night. It's so horrible. I don't know what to do. I haven't left my room.

I watched TV with Todd and Jami until midnight. Everyone else was out. I went to bed and was woken up by Ted. He was on top of me. He was heavy and his breath smelled like beef jerky and beer. He ripped my pajama bottoms off and raped me.

I don't know what to do. What if he tries to do it again?

*Thursday, January 4, 1995, 9:50 P.M.*

They don't believe me! No one believes he hurt me. The police aren't doing anything. Everyone's mad at me. Mrs. Abbott refuses to talk to me. I'm staying in my room, except for school. I can't live here anymore.

Story stopped reading and took a deep breath. She wondered what would have happened if Kevin had refused to stop kissing her that night they'd gone out. Would she have been able to tell her parents and call the police like Zana had? Would they have believed her if he had forced himself upon her?

She decided not to tell Whitney and Erica exactly what had happened. She just said, "We made out and he took me home."

She wasn't sure what Kevin had told his friends, but she suspected he'd said something more, because now boys were constantly coming up and talking with her. However, the girls were keeping their distance.

Even Jake had finally taken notice of her. He'd stopped by her locker to talk a few times in the past week, and he'd even mentioned the winter dance. He didn't exactly ask her to go with him, but at least it was clear he knew about it.

Erica and Whitney conjectured that Story's newfound popularity with the guys was because of Kevin's acceptance of her.

Story wasn't so sure. She didn't have much experience with boys, and had only made out with a few guys up to that point. She wanted to give him the benefit of the doubt. Maybe Kevin didn't kiss and tell, and the other kids only knew what they saw in the restaurant.

Story had given up hope of going to the dance and had even promised her parents that she would stay home for a family board game night when Jake cornered her at her locker.

"Are you going with anyone to the dance on Friday?" he asked.

Story shook her head. "Not yet."

"Would you like to go with me?"

"Absolutely." She smiled broadly.

"Okay, then. See ya'." He grinned, then left her standing by her locker while he rushed down the hall to his next class.

She let out a whoop and dashed to her history class, excited to tell her friends the big news.

***

*Monday, January 8, 1995, 6:50 P.M.*

I ran away from the Abbotts' house. No one would talk to me anymore. When there was no place set for me at the dinner table on Saturday night, I packed up my stuff and called the convenience store where Dad works. He was just getting off work.

I asked him to pick me up at the McDonald's near where I was staying. I didn't tell him why I was leaving, and he didn't ask.

I filled 2 garbage bags with clothes and brought my school backpack filled with accumulated food. I left out the back door while they were still finishing dinner. I walked the half mile to McDonald's and used some saved lunch money to buy a hamburger and fries. I ate while I waited for him to come get me.

After sitting there until almost 10 P.M., Dad finally showed up. He staggered into the restaurant—clearly on drugs.

The manager was getting ready to close up and told us to leave. I didn't want Dad to drive in that condition, so we slept in his beat-up old car that night. The next morning, we drove to what looked like a condemned house. Dad is living there with 5 other junkies. There's no electricity or water. It's filthy. I've been sleeping in the car.

*Wednesday, January 10, 1995, 4:45 P.M.*

I've been mostly staying in the car and eating from my food stash when Dad's in the house or off looking for more drugs. It turns out that he's only working 2 shifts a week at the convenience store. Apparently, he's managed to clean himself up for that. But I doubt he'll last much longer.

I've been able to keep my food stash hidden from Dad. If I told him about it, he'd share it with the people in the house and there'd be no food for me. There's a garden hose at the house next door. After the family leaves for the day, I use it for drinking water and to wash up. I wish I could take a shower. I'm using my bathrobe as a blanket and sleeping in the backseat of the station wagon, which smells of cigarette smoke.

*Monday, January 15, 1995, 4:30 P.M.*

I'm now enrolled in school, which will allow me to eat breakfast and lunch there. By Saturday, my food stash was gone, so I've been eating only the dollar hot dogs Dad gives me each night. He probably thinks that's all I've been eating.

I took some placement tests this morning. The school administrator said that a twelve-year-old doesn't belong in 8th grade, but my straight As in 7th and 8th grade convinced her that she could be wrong. I scored so high on the tests that she recommended I be in 9th grade. I'm taller than most of the students in junior high, but she's concerned that I'm not emotionally mature enough for the social aspects.

I asked her to please assign me to 9th grade classes, because I want to finish school as soon as possible.

She said that it's okay as long as I'm in junior high and not in high school. She's concerned about such a young girl with the older kids.

I hope I can graduate from high school in 2 years. Maybe I can go to college far away from Dad and his druggie friends.

## Chapter Nineteen

Jake led Story into their school's Winter Wonderland dance forty minutes late. She'd been pacing for at least a half hour, waiting for him to pick her up. When he had, he'd refused to come in to meet her parents.

"We're late already," he said.

She grabbed her sweater and ran out the door.

They rode to the dance in his large Ford truck. She was relieved she hadn't worn a short dress. At least her maxi-length white dress didn't ride up too far as she stepped into the vehicle.

He seemed agitated on the way there. He kept flipping stations on the radio and fidgeting with his hair, which was now a few inches longer than it had been during football season.

"Are you okay?" she asked. She wondered if his behavior was somehow related to that boy's drowning last summer. Maybe seeing her reminded him of it.

He nodded.

When he finally found a parking place, he paused and took a deep breath. He turned to her and asked, "Will you please kiss me?"

She'd never heard of a boy asking for a kiss before. Didn't they just lean in and go for it? She interpreted his question and his nervousness as good manners. He wasn't like Kevin. She let him kiss her.

At first, he was gentle and tentative, then he pressed his tongue into her mouth and pulled her close to him with his muscular arms. After about ten minutes of kissing, she suggested they go inside to the dance.

He reluctantly agreed.

She found her friends, who questioned her tardiness. She simply raised her eyebrows in response. She didn't want to tell them how uncomfortable she was feeling with her date. Instead, Story pasted a smile on her face and moved to the rhythm of the music until Jake asked her to dance.

The other kids were dancing apart to the upbeat music while Jake drew her in for a slow dance and make out session. She could feel the heat in her face and wondered when a chaperone would interfere.

No one did.

They continued to make out in front of everyone for another song.

She pulled away and said she needed to use the bathroom, where she sat in a stall with her face in her hands. She didn't have enough experience with boys to understand what was going on. Did all of them want to make out all the time? She'd hoped they would talk about their feelings first—get to know each other.

"Are you okay in there?" Erica called to her.

Story quickly flushed the toilet, wiped her tears with toilet paper, and yelled back, "Yeah, I'm fine."

"Jake is wondering where you are. He thinks you might have left."

Story went to the sink and washed her hands, then carefully dried them.

"What's up?" Erica asked.

She looked around to see if anyone could hear her. "I guess I'm not used to all this making out."

"Get used to it," Erica said. "I love it. Eric is such a good kisser."

Story attempted a smile as she walked with her friend back to the gymnasium where Jake was talking with a few football buddies. When he saw her, he approached and said, "Do you want to get out of here?"

Story nodded.

If the only dancing they were going to do was making out, she'd rather not dance. She followed him back to his truck. This time, he helped her up on her side first before getting in himself. Maybe he was a gentleman after all.

Within minutes, he was kissing and groping her, tugging at her clothes.

She kept inching away from him until he had her against the passenger side door.

A clear thought finally came to her head. *This is* not *what I want.*

"No. Stop it." Then, in a much louder voice, she said, "Take me home."

"Baby, I'm doing what you like," he cooed. "Come on." He put his hand on her breast.

"Stop it!" She swatted his hand away.

She opened the truck door, jumped out, and ran back to the gymnasium as fast as she could.

Story didn't look behind her to see if Jake had followed her in. She went straight to the girls' bathroom and splashed water on her face over and over again in an effort to wash away the events of the night. Whitney came in just as she was drying her face.

"Where's Jake?" she asked.

Story felt a wave of emotion wash over her. Tears welled in her eyes and she couldn't find the words. Whitney enveloped her in a hug.

"It's okay," she said. "Do you want a ride home?"

Story nodded. She didn't need Jake when she had her best girlfriends.

***

*Sunday, February 5, 1995, 8:05 P.M.*

On Friday, the police raided the house and arrested everyone, including Dad. I was at school and didn't find out about it until I got back to the station wagon, which was parked down the street so as not to attract attention.

Chuck, one of the guys who had been living in the house, was waiting for me. He'd left to get a pack of cigarettes and when he'd returned, the police were leading everyone out in handcuffs. He suggested I stay put until Dad is released.

I nodded. If I managed to move the car myself, Dad might not be able to find me.

I thanked Chuck and waited for him to walk away before opening the car door. I don't trust anyone.

I don't think I'll be able to sleep tonight. I'm scared. I don't usually turn my flashlight on in the car after it gets dark, but the only thing that will calm me down is writing at night.

I talked to Chuck again today. He said that the court hearing will probably be tomorrow. He thinks that bail will be set and Dad will be released.

I shook my head and argued that Dad doesn't have any money.

Chuck put his grimy hand on my shoulder and said that a bail bondsman will probably help.

After feeling his hand on my shoulder, it made me too uncomfortable to want to stay on this street. There isn't much gas in the tank, but I was able to move the car a few streets down. It took me quite a while to park, but at least Chuck doesn't know I'm here.

*Monday, March 13, 1995, 6:22 P.M.*

It's been a long time since I felt like writing. Dad has finished his court-ordered community service. He's sleeping in doorways. I'm still sleeping in the car.

Dad stands at a busy intersection for a few hours every other day with a cardboard sign that reads: "Hungry. Daughter to feed."

I think he makes as much as $100 every day, but I'm not seeing much of it. It's going to his drug habit. Since he's been begging for money, he's been able to buy heroin. I'm not absolutely sure of this, but I caught him injecting his toes and his legs a few times. I heard him call it *smack* and *tar*.

He gives me $20 here and there. I saved up the money and was able to use it to join a YMCA a few blocks away, so I can use the bathroom and take showers. I swim in the pool after school every day. It beats hanging out in the car all the time.

I usually study in the lounge during the evenings. One day when Dad didn't seem too out of it, I asked him to move the car so it's closer to the YMCA. Now, I spend all my free time before and after school there and only sleep in the car.

*Saturday, March 18, 1995, 7:15 P.M.*

I'm sitting in the lobby at the YMCA. I'm starving. I haven't had any food since school lunch yesterday. I don't have any money and haven't seen Dad since Wednesday.

*Saturday, March 18, 1995, 7:45 P.M.*

The Y closes soon. I'm so hungry. I filled my water bottles up. Maybe I'll be able to sleep if I lay on my stomach. It dulls the hunger pangs.

*Sunday, March 19, 1995, 11:55 A.M.*

It was hard to sleep last night. This morning, I walked a few miles to the Hope Mission where they serve free breakfast on Sundays. I stood in line with about 50 other homeless people, including some children.

They gave me pancakes with syrup, fruit cocktail, and orange juice. I ate fast and was still hungry afterwards, but now I feel better.

As I was walking out, a lady was handing out loaves of bread and gave me one. I thanked her. At least I can eat bread tonight.

Story swallowed hard after reading about Zana's struggles. She could hardly remember a time when she'd truly felt hungry. She'd say she was starved if she felt the beginning of the slightest hunger pang. She freely threw food away when it didn't meet her high standards. Last night, she'd complained to her mom that the gravy wasn't hot enough and she preferred creamed corn to green beans. Half of her meal had gone in the garbage disposal. She thought nothing of spending money on a fashion magazine or a few Blockbuster movie rentals when a homeless person with an outstretched hand stood outside. Story had seen lines of people waiting for a meal at a nearby church.

She wondered what she could do to help. She returned to Zana's diary with a heavy heart.

*Wednesday, April 12, 1995, 7:25 P.M.*

Mrs. Hoffman, my Language Arts teacher, asked me to stay after class today. She thinks I'm depressed and wants to talk to Dad.

That would really make me depressed.

I promised to see the school nurse, but I just don't have the energy yet. I skipped swimming and have been sitting here in the YMCA lounge all afternoon. I fell asleep for a little while.

*Saturday, April 15, 1995, 5:30 P.M.*

Dad gave me $45 in crumpled dollar bills. I didn't ask him where he got it, but it was probably from begging. I used most of the money to pay my dues for April at the YMCA.

I feel a little better now. I was worried they'd cancel my membership and not let me in here anymore.

When I paid with the money, the lady looked concerned and asked me a bunch of questions. Next time, I'll try to get someone to give me a $20 bill. I don't like answering questions. There's no way I'm going back to foster care.

***

Story had gotten the idea to join the YMCA from Zana's diary. Not only was the Y a place to get fit, but she'd heard they occasionally gave free meals to the homeless. Maybe, she could help. She was sick of hanging out with Whitney and Erica, who now both had boyfriends. Whenever they got together, they never talked about anything else. After her experiences with Kevin and Jake, Story didn't want anything to do with boys—at least for a while. She didn't want to go to prom and if she were asked, she'd have to think long and hard about whether she was willing to subject herself to another evening of humiliation.

In addition to her resolve to help feed the homeless, she planned to focus on getting fit, graduating with the highest GPA possible, and getting accepted by one of her top choice universities. She'd applied to Stanford, Harvard, and Yale with the same attitude one has when purchasing lottery tickets. More realistic choices were UCLA, USC, University of Washington, and Oregon State University. She'd also applied to a handful of smaller, private schools that seemed to accept some students with less stellar grades and test scores. She'd applied to a few schools for their beautiful location, too—University of Hawaii, Cornell, Notre Dame, and the University of Colorado at Boulder.

Now that Whitney and Erica were busy with their boyfriends, Story ate lunch with a few students from her history class, whom she'd worked on a group project with. Leon was one of the top students academically in their class. He had already been accepted to MIT and was waiting to hear from a few more universities before making a decision. Penny wanted to be a medical doctor and had the grades she needed. She didn't want to talk about acceptance letters, because she was afraid she'd jinx it. Randy was new to their school, because his dad was in the military. He wasn't a top student, but he liked military history and planned to follow in his father's footsteps.

Story liked talking to Randy about World War II. He had a different perspective from what she'd been studying. She wondered if she should consider a military or even law enforcement career—maybe in the CIA or FBI. Randy was the only one she felt comfortable discussing these ideas with. Whatever she proposed, he responded enthusiastically.

***

*Tuesday, June 13, 1995, 7:05 P.M.*

A lot has happened since I last wrote. I'm no longer living in the car. It got towed. We couldn't afford to pay the fees, but I was able to get my clothes, which are now in a duffle bag I bought for $3.00 at Goodwill. School is out for the summer. I got all As and a B+ in science.

Dad has started giving me at least half of his begging money when I sit on the ground next to him. We've rented a room in a building that used to be an old motel. It's run down—there's no hot water and the sink doesn't work, but at least it's a roof over our heads. The coils from the old mattress poke into my back at night. The old TV doesn't work and there's no heat or air conditioner.

When Dad doesn't come home, I'm scared being here alone. I hear people yelling, things crashing, and sometimes, I hear gunshots. When he's here, it's scary, too. Strung-out drug addicts knock at the door and he lets them in. Sometimes, they sleep on the floor, on the chair, or with Dad in his bed.

*Wednesday, June 20, 1995, 8:15 P.M.*

I'm sick of begging to get money. We bought a folding camp chair at Goodwill for a few bucks, so I have a place to sit and read library books while Dad holds up the sign. I wear sunglasses and a hat and hold my book over my face as much as possible. Sometimes, men yell, "Get a job," or something crude about me. Then Dad gets mad and chases after them.

One time, he got in a fight with a truck driver. A policeman saw the fight and came over to break it up. I thought Dad was going to be arrested again, but he was let go. Later, Dad said that if it weren't for me sitting there, he would have been put in the slammer. Now, Dad will never go begging without me.

*Saturday, June 23, 1995, 8:30 P.M.*

I've been saving as much money from begging as I can. I have to hide the money so Dad doesn't find it. A few nights ago, he was rummaging through my duffel bag, looking for money. I usually plant a few dollars in there, so he thinks he's found my stash, and then he'll either go to bed or leave to get drugs.

I keep my real money stash in the lining of my bathrobe, which I sleep with like a security blanket. Dad hasn't questioned me about this. I thought about putting the money under my pillow or mattress, but I've caught Dad looking there when I've walked from the bathroom in the middle of the night. I put my robe on when I use the bathroom.

In the morning, when I take a cold shower, I move half the money from my robe and divide it between my pockets and my backpack. If Dad finds any of the money, at least he won't get all of it. I've saved $183.42 so far.

*Sunday, August 6, 1995, 9:10 P.M.*

I'm sick of this summer already. Every day: beg, sit in a dreary room, and watch Dad fall apart even more.

The good things about school starting:

1. Breakfast and lunch;

2. No more begging (hopefully);

3.Something to do besides sitting around;

4. New friends;

5. Learn interesting things;

6. Maybe I'll get to swim or do other sports activities.

The bad things about school starting:

1. Less money (I'm not helping Dad beg);

2. I'm not around to prevent Dad from taking drugs during the day;

3. Without money, we might not be able to live here;

4. I'm going to a new school where I don't know anyone;

5. I'm worried about being teased and bullied, because I'm poor;

6. I can't sleep well at night because of all the noise in this place. I won't be able to take naps during the day;

7. It's going to be hard to study here. I don't have a desk and people are yelling and screaming all the time. I hear bouncing on beds, headboards pounding against walls, and dogs barking at all hours.

***

The restaurant was packed. Story's section was almost twice as large as usual, and she now knew what "being in the weeds" meant. She took a few deep breaths, smiled broadly, and approached table eleven. The couple had put down their menus and were clearly ready to order food. They didn't have water, bread, or cocktails.

"Good evening. I'm Story, and I'll be your server this evening. Would you like to start off with drinks?" she said in the friendliest voice she could muster.

"Oh, are you Story Sanchez?" the woman asked.

"That's me." Story smiled.

"Our son talks about you all the time," the man said.

"Oh?"

"Our son, Randy Pullman."

"Really?" Story's eyes widened. She hadn't seen him since they'd graduated. They'd hung out at the graduation party together and promised to keep in touch. "What's he up to?"

"He's been working out—getting ready for boot camp," his dad said.

Story bit her lip. The US was involved in wars on two fronts—Iraq and Afghanistan. Her chest felt heavy at the thought of Randy being deployed in the midst of all the violence and uncertainty.

"We're worried, too," his mother said. "I'll tell him to call you before he leaves."

"Please do. I'd love to talk with him."

Story missed her friend. They'd grown close the last

few months of the school year. They had been in three of the same classes, were locker neighbors, ate lunch together, and usually studied together after class or talked on the phone. She'd been so busy with her new job and getting ready to attend the University of Hawaii—one of her beautiful location schools—she hadn't thought much of anything else.

Randy had laughed when she'd told him that if she couldn't get into Stanford or Harvard, at least she could enjoy the ambiance while she studied. Her parents weren't completely opposed to the idea. They looked forward to visiting her.

Randy's parents left her a big tip and promised to have their son call her the next day. Story couldn't wait to catch up. Maybe they could go out for a celebratory pizza.

***

*Saturday, August 12, 1995, 8:35 P.M.*

A weird thing happened to me today. I'm not really sure how to explain it. I was looking for Dad, as I often do. I haven't seen him for about three days. So, I left our room and was walking around the neighborhood when a bald man, wearing a lot of gold jewelry, asked me my name.

I ignored him and kept on walking.

He grabbed my arm and said I wasn't safe walking alone on the street.

I tried to get away from him, but he was too strong. He said that a pretty girl like me could make a lot of money.

I didn't answer.

He yanked me towards a car, but then a group of people walking down the street seemed to scare him. He let me go, jumped in the car, and drove away.

An older man asked me if I was okay.

I nodded and walked quickly to our room. I think the guy is a pimp. I've seen him talking to some women who Dad said are prostitutes. I'm not walking on that street anymore.

*Tuesday, August 15, 1995, 7:15 P.M.*

Dad finally came home. While I walked with him to a soup kitchen, I saw the bald man watching me. He was leaning against a black car.

I quickly turned away and told Dad to walk faster. By the time we reached our destination, I was in tears. I cried all through breakfast.

Dad kept asking me what was wrong.

I finally told him that I'm scared, that there's a man following me. We can't go to the police or I'll probably go to foster care again. The only solution is to move.

Story felt her heart race as she read about Zana's scare. She wondered if she'd be able to sleep that night. She'd probably be finished reading the diary if it didn't cause her so much anxiety. It seemed that every time she picked it up to dive into the girl's adventures, another horrible thing was happening to Zana. Story sighed and closed her eyes.

"Story!" Her mom called, interrupting her thoughts. "Phone call!"

After Story picked up the phone in the kitchen downstairs, she immediately recognized the caller's voice. It was Randy.

"I miss you," he said after they talked about boot camp.

Story smiled. "Me too, you."

"Will you promise to write?"

She nodded and then realized he couldn't see her. "Of course."

That night, when Story turned off the light and pulled her covers up to her chin, she smiled. She wondered if there might be a guy out there for her after all. Could it be Randy?

***

*Wednesday, September 13, 1995, 9:25 P.M.*

It's been a month since I've written anything. Dad refused to move. I've stayed in our room until school started.

Sometimes, he disappears for days. I've been so hungry, but terrified to leave the room. I thought the man would be waiting outside for me.

I had nightmares about the bald man attacking me. I've also been having nightmares about Ted. It got to the point that I wouldn't get out of bed unless I had to use the bathroom. I've gotten so skinny. I can see my ribs.

The day before school started, Dad forced me to get out of bed and walked with me to the soup kitchen. I ate until I felt sick. After lunch, Dad introduced me to Pastor Paul. He told me if I ever needed to talk to someone, he's there for me. *What?* I needed to talk to someone immediately. I didn't say anything.

Dad made me go to school the next day. I've been eating at school and I'm not as depressed. I'm taking the school bus and if I'm too scared to walk to the stop, I've been using the money I saved to take a taxi.

*Saturday, September 16, 1995, 5:33 P.M.*

I've noticed that most adults find life so difficult that they try to escape by all sorts of means. When Mom was alive, she and Dad spent all their time swimming, biking, and running—probably to avoid thinking about their money problems. Dad started using drugs in order to escape his grief. I've watched foster parents disengage from life by eating, watching TV, drinking alcohol, smoking, or shopping.

Kids do it, too. Kids avoid problems and responsibility by playing video games, sleeping, vegging out in front of the TV, or talking on the phone with their friends. I read books all the time to escape life. If I weren't so afraid to leave this room, I'd swim, bike, and run like Dad and Mom did. What would happen if I faced my problems and tried to find a way to make my life better, rather than avoid them? I'm only 12, but I think I can figure out some ways to get out of this mess if I stop doing what Dad's doing. I'm not taking drugs, but I'm doing lots of things to hide from life.

## Chapter Twenty

Story used what islanders call a "rubber slippah"—a flip flop—to smash a small cockroach crawling up the wall in her dorm room. She'd been in Honolulu for almost a month and was still scared to get out of bed during the night to use the bathroom she and her roommate shared with four other freshmen. When she turned on the light, there would sometimes be a huge cockroach, called a "B-52," because they could fly.

She didn't mind the geckoes. They were cute and ate the cockroaches. Her roommate, Leilani, was from upcountry Maui and didn't understand what all the fuss was about. She'd grown up with big bugs and whenever Story complained, she'd tell her own stories of far creepier creatures.

Story was now used to her schedule. She had classes all day on Mondays, Wednesdays, and Fridays, and only one morning class on Tuesdays and Thursdays, allowing her to work a few shifts at the Kahala Mall at Starbucks.

Her parents didn't want her to work, because they wanted her to focus only on her schoolwork. She'd gotten used to earning pocket money, meeting interesting people, and pushing herself to learn new things. She'd applied to be a barista in order to learn how to make exotic coffee drinks.

Story wished she were a junior already so she could avoid taking the intro classes. She was anxious to delve into the higher-level history, political science, sociology, and psychology classes. Rather than wait to learn more advanced material, she decided to work on an extra credit special study project for each class. She knew this was a little over the top, but she had lots of time to spend in the library. She had no interest in obtaining a social life.

The only friendship she was focused on now, outside of her roommate and a handful of girls at the dorm, was with Randy Pullman by email and the occasional letter. He was in the middle of Army Basic Training at Fort Benning in Columbus, Georgia. He planned to go to college and become an Army officer in the future, but for now, he was anxious to serve in Iraq. Story remembered he'd become obsessed with serving after 9/11. It showed in his mannerisms over a series of dinners, hikes, and phone calls they'd had in July and early August, before they'd both packed up and moved to begin their future lives, as they'd called it.

She couldn't help but worry about him.

***

*Wednesday, November 15, 1995, 8:30 P.M.*

In the past 2 months, I've made some changes. I decided to stop being so afraid of everything and to do more. I've made a few friends at school. With some of the money I've been saving, I bought a used bike. I ride to and from school, and everywhere else on it.

I joined our school's swim team. I'm so much younger than the other girls, but I'm one of the fastest at freestyle and butterfly. I'm in French class and joined the French club. After my school activities, I go to a nearby library and study until closing.

Dad hasn't asked why I'm never home, but he seems to be doing well enough begging for money. He's been giving me about $5 a day—sometimes more. I spend a few dollars on dinner and try to save as much as possible.

*Sunday, November 19, 1995, 9:10 P.M.*

This morning, I helped my new friend Amy with her paper route. I had to get up in the middle of the night and ride my bike a few miles to meet up with her.

We were able to finish the route quickly and she gave me half the money she earned for the morning.

Her parents are hoping that I can take over the route for a few days each week to allow her to sleep in and go to church on Sundays. I'd rather work and make my own money than rely on Dad.

*Sunday, November 26, 1995, 8:15 P.M.*

I sort of messed up. Amy warned me not to slam newspapers against doors. She said that it's loud, wakes up people, and they get mad. I did the paper route alone this morning for the first time. I used the technique Amy taught me. I toss the paper gently onto the porch so it makes a dull thud. This sound bothers some homeowners, but it's not so loud that they complain.

I think I got lazy or tired when I got to the big white house on the corner. I threw the paper and it slammed against the door.

Before I could ride away, a woman came out in her bathrobe. I froze.

Instead of yelling, she asked me to come and talk to her. She said her name is Felicia and asked for my name. I told her.

She explained how Amy tosses the newspaper, instead of slamming it against the door.

I apologized and promised that I would be more careful next time. She smiled and gave me a $1 tip. I don't get why she gave me money when I messed up.

Story put the diary down. Her eyes were heavy from jet lag. She'd flown in from Florida the night before, and even though it was only 6 P.M. in Honolulu, it was midnight in Orlando. Anthony and Brooke had gotten married in the Morocco Pavilion at Epcot Center with a small wedding party of their immediate family members and a few close friends.

The best part was spending the entire day of the wedding at Epcot, and the day after at Disney World. Anthony and Brooke had joined in on the fun on both days, starting their life together magically. Story wondered if Zana would ever experience the pure joy that she'd had during her long weekend adventure. She kept reading.

*Wednesday, December 13, 1995, 7:05 P.M.*

Amy's parents made her give up her paper route so I'm doing it alone as of last week. It's nice to have money coming in. I paid for a plumber to fix the sink in the bathroom, and I bought a microwave oven with the money I accumulated from Dad. I'm now saving up for a small refrigerator.

Dad hasn't been home for over a week and doesn't know about my new job. I have to leave here at about 2:45 A.M. to pick up and prepare the papers. The first day I did the route alone, I didn't get done until after 7 A.M., and I got a few complaints.

This morning, I finished before 6 and even talked to that woman at the white house—Felicia—for a few minutes. She gave me a $1 tip again today. She's really nice.

*Saturday, December 16, 1995, 6:55 P.M.*

Felicia invited me to come into her house and eat breakfast this morning. Since her house is the last one, I was able to do it. She cooked banana pancakes and crispy bacon. It was the best breakfast ever!

Felicia said she was surprised I ate so much, so quickly. She hopes to put "some meat on my bones."

That's fine with me. Some of the kids at school tease me that I look like a beanpole. Maybe they'll stop saying that if I eat breakfast at Felicia's house more often.

*Sunday, December 24, 1995, 5:20 P.M.*

I'm delusional. I thought Dad might change. He was acting normal for a few weeks. I came home after my paper route this morning and the microwave I bought was gone. No more heated soup or hot pockets for dinner.

He'd sold it for drugs—just like everything else I get. If I buy a cute necklace and lay it on the dresser, it's gone.

I'm so sick of it. I work my butt off delivering newspapers and it doesn't get me anywhere. Foster care scares me. Living in this filthy room is more than depressing. Half the time, strangers are sleeping on the floor or are in bed with Dad. When he lets a man stay here, I can't sleep for fear I'll be attacked in my sleep. One time, one of his friends who was high on drugs tried to make a move on me.

I kicked and punched him until he said he was sorry. Dad told him he should leave. Christmas is tomorrow. There won't be any presents, tree, or hot meal. It'll be just another day.

***

It felt good for Story to be home and sleep in her own room. At dinner, she marveled at the mashed potatoes and gravy. She'd been eating rice with almost every meal since she'd been living in Hawaii. Even though she seldom took baths when living at home, she treated herself to a bubble bath—something she couldn't do even if she wanted to in the dorms, where there were only showers.

"How are you fitting in?" Dad asked.

"Everyone thinks I'm a local with my darker skin, brown eyes, and long black hair. I've had a few Starbucks customers ask if I'm Hawaiian." Story laughed. "Once they hear me mispronounce the Hawaiian words, they know I'm a *mainlander*."

Story joined in a family game of Monopoly. Anthony and Brooke were visiting, too, and Brooke was just beginning to show. Their baby was due in early June. Story couldn't wait to be an auntie.

"A little boy or girl?" Kimberly asked.

Anthony and Brooke laughed and together said, "One, two, three," and then pulled up their sweaters to reveal pink t-shirts underneath.

Everyone jumped up and hugged them.

"You must have known you'd be asked," Story said.

"Of course!" Anthony beamed.

When they went upstairs to their rooms, with Anthony and Brooke staying together in Kimberly's room while Kimberly bunked with Betsy, Story said, "My, how times change."

"You're not kidding me." Anthony winked.

Story wondered if their parents had ever found out that they'd been living together. She wouldn't know unless she asked them, but she wouldn't betray her brother's confidence. She wondered what their reaction would be in case she ever shacked up with a future boyfriend.

Back in her room, which looked just like she'd left it, Story lay on her bed with Maggie curled under her arm like old times. She'd missed her cat terribly and insisted that her mom intermittently give her updates while she was away. Her mom consistently said, "Maggie's fine" or "Maggie misses you."

Sitting on her bed, Story suddenly had the urge to call Whitney or Erica, whom she hadn't talked to since graduation. Last Story heard, Whitney was attending the hotel restaurant management program at Washington State University and Erica was hoping to get into the nursing program at University of San Diego. She heard that both of them had broken up with their high school boyfriends. She wondered what their lives were like now.

Story opened her laptop and checked her email. Just as he'd hoped, Randy was deploying to Iraq at the beginning of the year and was completing pre-deployment training somewhere in Texas. She smiled when she saw an email from him.

> *Hi Story,*
>
> *I'm exhausted. Long day. I hope you're snuggling with Maggie in your own bed tonight. I'm sleeping on an uncomfortable cot with a scratchy blanket, of course. Now, time for bed. I'll try to call you before we fly out. I miss our talks.*
>
> *Aloha,*
>
> *Randy*

Ever since she'd been in Hawaii, Randy had been ending his emails with "Aloha." She wasn't sure if he meant "goodbye," or "love," as the word meant both, among other things. She hoped he meant love, because that's what she meant when she used it in her emails to him.

Before Story climbed into bed, one of Zana's diaries caught her eye. It had been months since she'd read any entries. Even though they made her feel gratitude for her own life and inspired her to be better, they were often gut-wrenching to read. Story had to be in just the right mood. She reached for the diary and opened it where she'd placed her favorite floral bookmark.

*Monday, February 5, 1996, 8:00 P.M.*

Even though home life sucks, I'm doing well in school. A counselor noticed my perfect grades and asked to meet with Dad and me. I didn't bother to tell him about the meeting and went without him. I told Mrs. Trigg that Dad was working. She bought the excuse and asked lots of questions about my future plans.

I told her that I want to get through school as fast as possible. I left out the part about being miserable in my home life and wanting to get away from Dad and his druggie friends.

I think she expected me to have bigger ambitions for myself. She asked me what I want to be when I grow up.

I stared at her for a long moment, then blurted out that I want to be a lawyer. I don't know why I said it. Maybe because I liked Mr. Kekoa so much and he's a lawyer. Or, maybe because I ate breakfast at Felicia's house yesterday and she told me that she's a lawyer.

Mrs. Trigg asked me why I want to be a lawyer.

I said, "I want to help people." What I really want to do is help myself.

She seemed satisfied and asked if I'd be interested in taking AP classes, taking college classes, or graduating early.

I said that my only interest would be to graduate as early as possible. I'm not sure I'll go to college. I want to graduate and work to support myself.

Before I left her office, I asked her how long before I could graduate.

She smiled and said maybe I can graduate a year early.

I've skipped a few grades, but even so, it looks like I still have 3.5 years of school left. This doesn't help me at all.

*Wednesday, March 15, 1996, 7:15 P.M.*

Dad's in jail again. He might be there for a while, because he was charged with using a stolen credit card. I've been using my money from my paper route to pay for our room, but we're at least a month behind on rent.

The landlord, Mr. Kiley, knocks on the door a lot and asks to speak to my dad.

I tell him I don't know where he is. I think Mr. Kiley feels sorry for me. He keeps telling me to let him know when Dad comes home. Every time he stops by, I hand him a few more dollars to put towards rent but Mr. Kiley hands it back to me. He tells me to buy food.

I need another job or I'm going to be homeless again.

*Monday, April 10, 1996, 7:10 P.M.*

Dad came back on Friday. There were eviction notices all over the door. Instead of scoring drugs right away, he begged on the busiest street corner all weekend.

I don't think we're completely caught up with rent, but the eviction letters were taken off the door. I'm so angry at Dad. I'm not talking to him unless I have to.

*Saturday, April 15, 1996, 5:35 P.M.*

My heart feels like it's beating out of my chest. I can't believe I told her, but I did. It just poured out of my mouth. I wasn't thinking. When I finally realized what I did, it was too late.

I told Felicia everything.

She sat and listened. And nodded. She put her hand on my shoulder when I cried.

Mostly, I gave her my unfiltered version about Mom's death, Dad's drug use, foster homes, being raped, begging, taking care of myself, people sleeping in our room, hiding money, threats of eviction, my fears, and my wanting to escape. After I told her everything, she gave me a long hug.

She said, "Zana West, even though you've had many challenges, I know you'll make a success of your life."

***

The sun beat down, causing her bikini-clad body to glisten with sweat. Story took a sip from her water bottle. She was lying on a beach towel at San Souci Beach, reading her psychology textbook. She'd spent far too much time in libraries. It was time to feel the warmth of the sun, sand between her toes, and tropical breezes.

Even though finals weren't for another few weeks, she felt ready. She'd earned a 3.9 on her first semester report card and she hoped she could do the same or better this semester. A few years ago, she'd struggled with getting Cs, and now she was a top student. It was amazing how things changed when she focused.

She felt that way about her love life, too. It wasn't long ago when she'd felt taken advantage of by high school boys and suffered from an undeserved reputation. There was no choice in her mind but to take a complete break from dating. She had decided just to be friends with boys, but now, she was in love for the very first time.

She smiled as she thought about Randy. He'd written her a long letter and in the last paragraph, he'd said:

> *We'll soon be ordered to go to the front line. I must admit, I'm scared. Not because of the danger of potential loss of life or limb. I'm scared because of the possibility I'll never again see you, hear your voice, or feel your touch. Story, I love you.*
>
> *I hope you feel the same way, but if you don't, that's okay, too. I hope that someday I'll*

*come home and we can be together.*
*I imagine our lives together—married, kids, careers, vacations, celebrations... However, even if you're just my friend, I'm happy.*

*Love,*

*Randy*

She'd literally jumped for joy upon reading his words. She hadn't wanted to admit her feelings for him to herself until she knew that he felt the same.

Story immediately emailed him to tell him she loved him, too.

And ever since that day, they'd been carrying on an overseas romance. As soon as he could take leave, he would come to Hawaii. Until then, she studied and dreamt of their future together.

***

*Sunday, April 16, 1996, 11:09 A.M.*

When I delivered Felicia's paper this morning, she came out and apologized for not having time to talk, but she handed me a brown paper bag and gave me a hug before I rode my bicycle away. In the bag were 2 hard-boiled eggs, a banana, an apple, a packet of cheese and crackers, a small carton of chocolate milk, and a few dollars.

A note from her said,

*Dear Zana,*

*Thank you for trusting me with your story yesterday. I want to help you, but I know how much you don't want to go back to foster care. Let me think about possible other solutions for you.*

*Let's talk later in the week.*

*Your friend,*
*Felicia*

I tried hard not to cry. Instead, I focused on biting my nails. When my thumb started bleeding, the tears began to flow.

*Thursday, April 20, 1996, 7:20 P.M.*

A few nights ago, Dad found most of the money I was saving and bought cocaine for a party he had in our room while I was there. He invited a half dozen addicts and while they snorted coke, he kept telling them how I was hiding money from my own dad and this is what I get for being so sneaky.

The other men in the room became aggressive and kept grabbing me.

I screamed as I tried to run away when a man tore my dress, leaving me in my bra and panties.

I thought the red-haired man was going to rape me, but he only pressed himself against me and told me to leave before something bad happened.

Dad was laughing the entire time.

I grabbed a blanket and hid in the stairwell all night. I couldn't go to school the next morning, because I didn't have clothes or my books. I've missed my paper route for two mornings, so I think I'm going to be fired.

Our place was completely trashed when I returned a few hours ago. I can't remember the last time I ate something. I can't stop crying. I don't know where Dad is. I hate him.

*Tuesday, June 13, 1996, 8:50 P.M.*

I've been too depressed to write. We got kicked out of the motel after Dad's cocaine party. I lost my paper route. We're now living in a damp basement room in a house. We share a bathroom with the other drug addicts renting rooms here.

I have to be super careful where I walk to avoid stepping on a discarded needle. Yesterday, I almost got poked when I grabbed a towel in the bathroom. I hate it here. I'm hungry. I'm bored. Dad sold my bike to pay for drugs. I want to die.

# Chapter Twenty-one

Story pulled her sweater tight around her body in an effort to warm up. Her blood had gotten thin from living in Hawaii and was no match for the hospital's air conditioner. She had flown all night to LA after receiving the call.

Now, she huddled with her dad, Kimberly, and Betsy in the waiting room as her mom underwent emergency surgery. The doctor had told them that heart attacks in women were harder to identify. Her mom had complained to her doctor about shortness of breath, nausea, and jaw and back pain. To everyone's surprise, she had been having a heart attack.

"What if Mom dies?" Betsy wailed.

"She'll be fine, sweetheart," Dad said, pulling her onto his lap.

Story bit her lip. A few friends from high school and college had lost their parents to cancer or heart attacks. She remembered how Zana's diary had started—her mom had died of a heart attack and she'd ended up homeless.

Tears began streaming down Story's face.

***

*Friday, June 17, 1996, 7:35 P.M.*

A lady gave me a packet of M&Ms at the soup kitchen tonight. She said she was saving them for me. The Hope Mission doesn't get a lot of kids. I think the women and their children are afraid to go there, because there are so many creepy men.

*Monday, June 20, 1996, 8:10 P.M.*

I wonder if foster care would be better than this. Baggy, the guy who lives in the room next to ours, has been groaning for about 3 hours. I have no idea where Dad has been for the last few days. I'm afraid to go to Hope Mission by myself. I'm afraid to leave the room. I'm hungry.

*Tuesday, August 8, 1996, 5:30 P.M.*

It's been a while since I've written. I've been doing odd jobs for Felicia around her house a few times each week. I clean, garden, wash her car, and hem her pants. I ran into her last month at the library, where I started going when it became unbearable living here.

She asked me if everything was all right and I burst into tears.

Ever since then, I go to her house on Saturday mornings for breakfast before spending the day doing chores for her. If there's more to do, I come back mid-week.

She asked me if I'm ready to go to foster care.

I shook my head. I told her that I'd rather get a job and live on my own.

Her eyes looked worried, but I don't think she's going to call child protection.

*Friday, August 12, 1996, 7:40 P.M.*

One of the men who lives here has been trying to get me to use drugs. He's super skinny and everyone calls him Pike. Maybe that's his last name.

Every time he sees me, he holds out his bong, some pills, or a bottle of beer and says, "You don't know what you're missing, Squirt."

I always shake my head and walk away without saying anything. I do know what I'm missing. There's no way I want to turn out like these losers. I've got to find a way to get out of here.

*Sunday, August 14, 1996, 5:20 P.M.*

I went swimming today for the first time in ages. It felt wonderful! I used some money I earned from working for Felicia to go to the public pool. I spent the day swimming laps and soaking up the sun. I bought a hot dog for lunch at the concession stand. I saw a few girls I've gone to school with and got a chance to catch up on some gossip about other kids. For a little while, I felt like a normal teenager.

*Wednesday, August 17, 1996, 8:25 P.M.*

Felicia wants to hire me to be a file clerk and runner at her law office during the school year. I'll work every day after school and will be putting documents in files, copying documents on their copy machine, making deliveries to other law firms, or going to court to file documents.

She said she usually hires someone older than me, but I've proven that I'm responsible. She gave me a bike she had stored in her garage.

I didn't see it there before, so I think she bought it for me. I don't know what I'd do without her. I wish I could live here until I graduate.

***

The flight back to Honolulu had a party-like atmosphere. Everyone seemed to be smiling, drinking Mai Tais, and playing the "halfway to Hawaii" game where people estimate the time when the plane reaches the geographical halfway point between takeoff and landing.

Story didn't feel like playing or joining in the cheer. She was happy to be going back to school, but wanted to stay home longer to help her mom while she recovered. She was getting better every day. She'd lost a lot of weight, though, and was weaker than before the surgery.

For the first time ever, Story began to appreciate what she had. Her parents argued like every married couple but stayed together. They had a nice house in a safe neighborhood and had every opportunity available to them. She sometimes wondered what it would be like if she was in Zana's shoes and had to struggle for everything she got. In so many ways, her life was the opposite of Zana's. Story's parents gave her money and didn't want her to work. She worked only because she wanted to, while Zana worked to survive.

The five-hour flight gave Story time to think about her life. She'd only seen Randy once since they'd declared their love to each other. He was only halfway done with his deployment and then he'd return to Fort Lewis, where he was stationed.

Whenever Story thought about following Randy around with the military, she became sick to her stomach. She had no interest in being a military wife. She wanted a career. She wanted to call the shots and not be subjected to the directive of a government agency.

Randy, on the other hand, had been waiting to serve in the military all his life. He wanted more than anything to follow in his dad's footsteps and become an officer. His mother was happy moving whenever they had orders to go—to Germany, Japan, Oklahoma, North Carolina, Puerto Rico—or, wherever.

Story bit her lip. The burning question was, what did she want to do with her life, and was that mission compatible with Randy's goals?

***

*Thursday, September 21, 1996, 9:00 P.M.*

I feel sort of happy. I'm not used to this feeling and it's so weird. For the last hour, I've been sitting on my bed, reading my social studies textbook, and noticed that my muscles in my chest feel relaxed. I put down my book and have been thinking about this. The good things: Dad has let me have this room to myself. He's sleeping on a bed in the downstairs common area. No one seems to care, and it gives me my own space. I'm eating breakfast and lunch at school and have money to buy something for dinner most nights. I have friends at school. They're older girls, but they're really nice—Melissa, Lisa, Kelly, and Crystal are my main group. The 5 of us eat lunch together.

I've gone over to Melissa's and Kelly's houses on the weekends to hang out. I love my after-school job. The people are nice and the work isn't too hard.

Felicia has helped me open a checking account at a local bank, so Dad won't steal my money. She had to pretend to be my guardian.

The bad things: Dad is worse than ever. The men who live in this house are in bad shape. Pike had an overdose. An ambulance came to the house and took him away. I haven't seen him since. He might be in the hospital. Or dead.

*Sunday, September 24, 1996, 7:35 P.M.*

Lisa had an afternoon birthday party at her house today. There were about 12 kids from school there. I bought her a bracelet and she really liked it. We played games, then ate cake and ice cream. I felt like part of the group. No one teased me about being tall and skinny. It was a fun day.

*Thursday, October 19, 1996, 8:10 P.M.*

I made a few mistakes at work. I hope Felicia isn't too mad at me. I misfiled a document so when she went to court, the document wasn't in her file.

Yesterday, I didn't make it to court in time to file a document that was due. I got there about 30 seconds too late. I don't think it was my fault, because Sabrina, the paralegal, didn't give me the document until 15 minutes before closing. I rode my bike as fast as I could.

*Monday, October 23, 1996, 9:25 P.M.*

Work went better today. I caught up on all the filing and asked Felicia if she wanted me to reorganize the storage room. She praised me and said she wished all of the employees had my initiative.

*Friday, October 27, 1996, 8:30 P.M.*

I'm going to a Halloween party with my friends tomorrow night, but I haven't had time to find a costume. I think I can make a Catwoman costume with black leggings, a long-sleeved black workout shirt, and my short black boots. I'll buy some cat ears and a black mask at the drugstore. I might have to make a tail.

Melissa is dressing up as Carmen Sandiego, Kelly will be Cher Horowitz from Clueless, and Lisa is going as Morticia from the Addams family. This is the first time I'm doing something fun for Halloween in years. I can't wait!

***

Professor Cole called Story into her office after class. In her experience from high school, this couldn't be good. However, her university grades were almost perfect. Maybe she'd done poorly on her last quiz and her professor wanted to get her back on the right track.

"Ms. Sanchez, I'm sure you're wondering why I asked to talk with you." Professor Cole's hands were in a steeple position as she sat behind her industrial school-issued metal desk.

Story nodded and hoped she'd get to the point soon. She had to get to her psychology class.

"There's an internship opportunity available at a law firm. My brother-in-law, Frank Gravelle, gives a few university students the opportunity to work in the litigation department of his firm each year, and usually asks me for recommendations." Professor Cole paused and wiped her glasses with a tiny cloth. "I'd like to recommend you, if that's okay."

Story felt her stomach flutter. "Absolutely. Thank you so much, Professor."

She had a hard time concentrating during her next class. She'd never thought about working at a law firm. She didn't think she was smart enough to be considered for such a job. The only thing she'd ever excelled at before was history, and lately, she'd done well in all her classes, because she'd been studying every free moment.

Later that afternoon as she was walking back to her dorm, Story felt like skipping or leaping into the air. She couldn't remember a time when she was more excited about anything.

# Chapter Twenty-two

*Tuesday, November 7, 1996, 9:15 P.M.*

Lisa found out about my home situation. I've been trying to keep it a secret from my friends, but somehow, she got my address and stopped by when I was at work. Dad was high on drugs and let her in for a few minutes until she felt so uncomfortable that she left.

The next day, she asked to talk with me privately. I begged her not to tell our other friends. She promised, but said they can't help me if they don't know.

Lisa said that her parents were divorced a few years ago, because her dad is an alcoholic. She lives with her mom, who remarried a nice guy about six months ago. She has two older stepbrothers. It's nice to have a friend to talk to about my situation, but I'm still embarrassed.

*Monday, November 20, 1996, 8:45 P.M.*

Lisa wrote me a note in math class today, inviting me to Thanksgiving dinner at her house. As soon as I read it, I wanted to jump up and down. I haven't had a nice Thanksgiving meal with a family since I was in foster care.

I told her, "Yes, I will absolutely come." Dad can go to the soup kitchen with his buddies.

*Thursday, December 14, 1996, 7:54 P.M.*

I've been spending a lot of time with Lisa since she found out about my home situation. Her parents are really nice to me.

Lisa invited me for a sleepover last Saturday. She has twin beds in her room with fresh-smelling sheets. The mattress felt like a cloud. I fell asleep immediately and didn't want to get out of bed in the morning.

After eating pancakes and berries for breakfast, Lisa told me that if I ever need a place to stay, I could come to her house.

*Wednesday, December 27, 1996, 9:00 P.M.*

I've been working more hours at the law firm over Christmas vacation and accumulating more money. I'm saving as much as I can. I call it my "Better Life Fund." Sometimes I call it my "Get Away from Dad Money" or my "Freedom Fund."

My plan is to be out of this house and away from Dad by the time I'm fifteen years old. I hope it doesn't take until I'm sixteen.

I've been talking to Felicia about becoming an emancipated minor. She'll represent me for free in the proceedings, but I need somewhere to go and a plan if this is going to work. She warned me that bringing my situation to the attention of the court could mean going back to foster care. That could be a disaster if I end up going to a different school or living too far away from the law firm to work. I'll have to be patient.

***

Story sat in a chair facing Frank Gravelle while he finished dictating a memo. She looked out the window at the view of Diamond Head and the ocean, imagining what it would be like to have an office like this and work as an attorney in the firm.

Frank put down his Dictaphone and turned his attention to her.

"Stephanie, you seem intelligent," Frank said. "You've showed up to work on time, you did everything we asked of you, and you get along with everyone—even some of our more challenging clients."

Story nodded.

Frank leaned forward. "Have you ever given any thought to going to law school?"

"I've enjoyed working here these last few months. Thank you for the opportunity, Mr. Gravelle."

"You didn't answer my question."

Story paused. "Yes, I'd like to go to law school. Very much."

"Well then. If you need a recommendation, you know where to get one." He stood up, reached out, and shook her hand firmly.

On her way out, Story stopped to say goodbye to Lori and Tom, the two attorneys she'd been assigned to help. They were in Lori's office, poring over papers strewn across her desk.

"I hope he was nice to you, or I'll kick his ass." Lori placed the documents she was holding onto a pile.

"Yeah, he said I should go to law school and he'll give me a recommendation." Story smiled.

"Are you kidding me?" Tom's eyes widened. "He never says that to interns. You should take that as a huge compliment."

"I do," Story said.

"You'd do great in law school." Lori stood up and gave her a hug. "After you graduate, you can get a good job at a much more civilized law firm than this one."

They laughed in unison.

***

*Sunday, February 4, 1997, 8:28 P.M.*

I had high hopes for 1997, but it's not turning out so well. I started feeling sick on December 30th—a bad sore throat and headache. I stayed in bed most of the time but didn't feel any better.

I couldn't go to school the next week, since my body ached so badly and I could barely swallow. Obviously, Dad wasn't looking after me.

Lisa came over one day to check on me. I don't remember much, but she told her mom about how sick I was, and they took me to a doctor. I was dehydrated and my temperature was 104 degrees! I was put in the hospital for about a week with strep throat. Apparently, I could have died.

*Monday, February 5, 1997, 7:10 P.M.*

I'm back to work and school now. Felicia is surprised that after my serious illness and hospitalization, I haven't been taken away from Dad and put into foster care again. I didn't tell her about how Lisa's family covered for me. The last few days I was in the hospital, Dad came to visit. He looked almost presentable. I have a feeling that Lisa's mom was behind that.

*Wednesday, April 24, 1997, 9:30 P.M.*

I've saved $1,009.62 in my "Get Away from Dad" fund. I'm not really sure how to use this money. I need a place to stay, food, and there are a bunch of other expenses I probably don't know about. I don't think a fourteen-year-old can live on her own very easily. I'll keep saving money until I figure it out.

Dad fell down some stairs—probably while he was high on drugs. He hurt his foot and arm. He doesn't have money to see a doctor, so he's limping around, drinking, and taking drugs for the pain.

I wonder if I should use some of my money so he can go see a doctor.

I think I should, but it's not like he's working and will be able to go back to work. I'm already paying for our room rent when he can't scrape up the money, which is most months. I pay for my clothes, food, and school supplies.

If Dad brings home some food, he always acts like he's some kind of hero. I'm sick of it. My friends' parents work all day and take care of their kids.

*Saturday, April 27, 1997, 8:07 P.M.*

Kelly and I went to see the movie *Fargo* today. It was so sick, with a guy killed in a wood chipper. I liked it and thought it was funny. Having only been to a movie theater twice before, this was a treat.

Movie popcorn is delicious. I wish I could see more movies, but I can't spend the money. After the movie, we went to the mall and met up with Melissa. They both bought new outfits at Nordstrom's. I tried on clothes and acted like I didn't find anything I liked. I think they know I was pretending, but I could have bought something if I wanted to.

***

Randy came back from deployment and wanted Story to quit school and move to Fort Lewis. Every time they talked on the phone, it turned into an argument. She, at least, wanted to finish her undergraduate degree at UH.

He didn't understand why it was so important to her. Didn't she want to get married and have kids? She didn't need a degree for that.

It got to the point that Story didn't want to talk to him. She wondered if they had anything in common. After all, they'd gotten to know each other when they were in high school. It'd been almost two years since they'd graduated, and they'd only seen each other a few times.

Story took a long walk on the beach—from San Souci to Magic Island. While she walked, she thought about her life and what she wanted for herself. She loved Hawaii and could see herself living and working here. She wasn't in a hurry to get married or start a family. She'd grown up with a stay-at-home mom who lived vicariously through her kids and husband. Then she'd had a heart attack and never gotten to fulfill any of her own dreams. Although Mom was doing well, she no longer had much energy for anything except talking on the phone and playing Canasta with her friends. That wasn't the life Story wanted.

If she were to be perfectly honest with herself, she wanted to go to law school—preferably at the

University of Hawaii. As she walked, she saw the outline of downtown high rises. What she really wanted was to be a Honolulu attorney. She'd gotten a taste for the profession during her internship. Zana's diary came to mind. She couldn't remember the last time she'd read an entry. She recalled how as an attorney, Felicia was able to help Zana. Story's heart swelled as she thought about what a difference she might make in other people's lives if she earned a law degree. When she returned to her apartment, she poured herself a glass of wine and relaxed on her sofa with Zana's diary.

*Wednesday, June 12, 1997, 9:17 P.M.*

I can't believe it's summer already. I've had the busiest school year ever. I got a B+ in calculus and a B in chemistry, but otherwise all As. I was super upset with the Bs, so I talked with my counselor.

She reminded me that I've skipped ahead two years and assured me that colleges will take that into account. I told her that I'm not good with math and science. She laughed and said that for me to get Bs in such advanced classes, that's really good. I'm not so sure.

*Saturday, June 29, 1997, 11:45 P.M.*

I went to a high school party with Melissa, Kelly, and Lisa. They were all drinking beer and getting drunk. I had a sip—it's gross—and held the beer, pretending to drink it. When no one was looking, I poured some of it out on the grass. I refuse to turn into my dad.

*Friday, July 5, 1997, 8:05 P.M.*

It's a long holiday weekend, because the law firm closed for the Fourth of July and today. My friends are all on vacation with their families. I think Dad is partying somewhere, because I haven't seen him for days.

I've been going to the pool and swimming laps. I bought a used triathlon bicycle and I've been riding it around town. Tomorrow, I think I'll go for a run. Maybe I can do a sprint triathlon before the end of the summer. The last time I did a triathlon was before Mom died, when I was a little kid.

I don't think the swimming or biking will be that bad, but my running needs some work. I've done some running in P.E., but nothing on my own.

*Friday, August 2, 1997, 7:45 P.M.*

My heart is pounding out of my chest. I'm racing in my first sprint triathlon in years tomorrow morning. Everything I need is in my backpack. I'll ride to the racecourse tomorrow morning at 4:30 A.M. I'm excited, but scared.

I didn't tell a soul that I'm doing this race. Melissa asked me if I could get together this weekend. I told her that I'm available on Sunday.

*Saturday, August 3, 1997, 8:05 P.M.*

I did it! I finished the race. There were five girls in my age group, and I came in third. I was ahead on the swim. I got passed by one of the girls on the bike and passed by the other on the run. They gave me a small trophy and I got a finisher's t-shirt.

I showed Dad the trophy. He got excited and gave me a hug. I think that's the first time he's hugged me in years.

# Chapter Twenty-three

It had been a long day. Story had competed in a biathlon—a swimming and running race at Magic Island. The 1K swim had been followed by a 5K run around the park. Ever since she'd moved out of the dorm and into her own apartment in Kakaako, she'd been running around Ala Moana Beach Park and swimming in the ocean for exercise.

When she'd heard about the race, she'd thought it would be fun. She had been right. Maybe someday she'd be like Zana and train for a triathlon.

She took a long swig of Gatorade, plopped down on the couch, and clicked on the TV. She needed to relax, because she had a long day at work tomorrow. She'd been working all summer at the family court's information desk, helping people navigate the court system. School would start again in a few weeks. She needed to focus solely on her studies during the academic year and prepare for the Law School Admissions Test.

The phone rang. She reluctantly dragged herself from the couch and picked it up after the fourth ring.

"Hey Mom, how are you?"

"I'm a little tired from playing cards with the girls, but otherwise good." She paused. "I called to find out how it went."

Story knew her mom wasn't talking about the biathlon.

"He took it well," Story said. "I think he saw the writing on the wall when I didn't go to Fort Lewis for the summer."

"How are you feeling, dear?"

Story sighed. She had been all cried out months ago when she'd come to the decision. During her procrastination phase, she'd mourned the loss of her relationship and was now ready to move on. "Surprisingly well. I'm actually relieved."

They changed the subject and her mom talked about Anthony and Brooke's visit with their little girl—Madison. Brooke was six months pregnant with a boy this time. Kimberly had just graduated high school and was getting ready to attend UC-Berkley, where she planned to study environmental engineering. Betsy was at cheerleading camp.

"Mom, before we get off the phone, there's something I want to tell you."

"Oh, no. What is it?" Mom asked.

"It's nothing bad. It's actually good." Story bit her lip. "You know how I've planned to teach history when I get out of school?"

"Uh huh."

"I don't want to do that anymore." She took a deep breath. "I want to go to law school."

"That makes sense with your internship and work at the court. You know your father and I support anything you want to do."

Story closed her eyes in relief. She could barely summon the courage to daydream about it. Now that she'd said it out loud, her plan seemed real.

"Thanks, Mom. I know."

***

*Sunday, August 4, 1997, 9:00 P.M.*

Melissa and I hung out today at her house by the swimming pool. I told her about the triathlon. She was super impressed and couldn't believe I'd been keeping it a secret. She wanted to hear all about it. Then, she told her mom and dad about my trophy.

Melissa is on our high school track team. She said she wishes she could do a triathlon, but she isn't a very good swimmer.

I'm surprised, because she has her own pool. If I had a pool, I'd swim every day.

*Thursday, August 15, 1997, 11:20 P.M.*

I'm still shaking. Trying to keep the ink on this page from smearing from my tears. Dad told me to take the bus and meet him at a building in an area I'm not familiar with at all. He said he wanted me to see an apartment.

I don't want to move schools, but I was sick of arguing with him, so I said I'd go after work.

I had some last-minute court filings to do, and I messed up the bus schedule, making me about thirty-five minutes late.

He wasn't there, but he's hardly on time for anything. I stood outside the building and waited.

I totally don't get what happened to me. I'm a kid!

Okay, I'm tall for my age—at five feet nine inches tall, but I'm skinny. I only weigh about 110 pounds. I have long black hair with short bangs—like a kid's. I was wearing a short skirt and wedge shoes, but my t-shirt had a cartoon rubber ducky on it. I don't wear makeup, because I'm only fourteen years old. I'm not sure why the men acted like they did. I don't understand it. Now, images of Ted keep flashing through my mind.

The two men pulled up next to me in a black sports car and said nasty things. They wanted to know how much I charge.

I ignored them and started to walk away, when one of the men jumped out of the car and grabbed me.

I tried to fight him off, but the other guy held my arms and put duct tape over my mouth, then rope around my wrists. They shoved me into the backseat of the car. One of them said they could get a good price for me, but the other one said he wanted me. They were arguing over loud music.

While they weren't paying attention, I was able to get loose from the rope. When they stopped for a red light, I opened the door and ran as fast as I could to the 7-Eleven on the corner. I didn't look back.

When I got inside the store, I still had tape over my mouth and I was crying. The store clerk called the police.

I talked to a policewoman and told her I'm eighteen years old. I didn't want them to send me to foster care. After I gave a report and described the men, two police officers gave me a ride home. I didn't want them to see where I lived, so I told them to take me to Lisa's house. I waved goodbye as they drove away, then I walked home.

I'm not telling anyone about this. Well, I might tell Dad and yell at him. It's his fault.

*Friday, August 16, 1997, 2:35 P.M.*

I called in sick today from the payphone at the corner gas station. I hate work. I hate Dad. I hate this place.

***

The bookstore was crowded as students bought books and school supplies for the new semester. Story had already selected the books needed for History of Southeast Asia and her Soc. 311 class—Survey of Social Inequality and Stratification. Next were the undergrad law classes, her first. The political science course was International Law, which required a textbook. The next was a business course.

"Excuse me, could you tell me where I can find the business law books?" she asked a clerk.

He pointed to three aisles down.

"Mahalo." She went in the direction he pointed and examined the shelves, but still couldn't find the books for her class.

"What are you looking for?" a tall Asian guy with a huge smile asked.

She smiled back. "Legal Environment and Business."

"Oh, I'm in your class." His smile grew bigger. "The books are hidden over here." He gestured, then laughed. "I can't ever find the books I need, either."

"Mahalo." She knelt down and took one of each.

"I'm Nick Lin." He reached out to shake her hand.

"Story Sanchez," she said as she held out her hand. She was surprised at his dry, firm grip. "Are you a business student?"

He nodded. "And, a wannabe law student."

"I'm history—and also a law student wannabe." She laughed. "I've never taken a law class before."

"Even the undergrad classes are tough."

They both headed to the counters to pay for their books. Story had brought a large backpack with wheels, because she knew she'd have a heavy load to carry back to her car in the parking lot blocks away.

While she was transferring the books from the cart to her backpack, Nick asked, "Would you like to join me for coffee?"

She hesitated a moment, then said, "Yes."

Over coffee at Starbucks in the adjacent campus center building, Story learned that Nick had grown up in Honolulu, his parents had immigrated from Taiwan, and he'd gone to a prestigious private school—Punahou. His parents expected him to be either a doctor or a lawyer.

"As their only child, I can't let them down. They both work two jobs and have made many sacrifices." His expression was serious for the first time since they'd met. "What about you? Why do you want to go to law school?"

Story hadn't ever thought through her reasons. "I'm not exactly sure why. In the past few years, a series of events have been leading me there." She paused and looked into her coffee cup. There was something about Nick that made her want to open up. "I found a girl's diary written over a span of many years. She's had a hard life and was helped by a female attorney. I know this sounds weird, but I think that if I become an attorney, I could help people like her."

"That doesn't sound weird at all." Nick grinned. "I wish I had a more altruistic reason."

Story smiled back. "You do."

***

*Saturday, October 12, 1997, 10:45 A.M.*

It's been months since I've written anything. The doctor said I'm depressed, but I think I'm starting to feel better. I had to take some pills for a while. I called in sick for a week. Then Felicia stopped by to check on me.

I wouldn't let her in, but agreed to ride my bike to her house. I told her what happened. She had tears in her eyes by the time I finished my story.

She took me to see a doctor, who examined me and said I was fine physically. He referred me to Dr. Dameron—a shrink.

Dr. Dameron said to call him Pat. At first, I saw him a couple times a week, and then once a week. Now, I see him once each month.

I wondered once who's paying for my treatment, but Felicia said not to worry about it. I haven't told Pat too much for fear he'll send me to foster care.

*Wednesday, October 16, 1997, 9:05 P.M.*

Pat said unless I open up to him, he can't do anything more to help me. He suggested I see someone else I might be more compatible with.

I shrugged my shoulders. Besides Felicia, I'm not telling anyone what's really going on. Dad is worse than ever. He's hanging around with an ugly, skinny woman named Lolly.

I walked into the bathroom and caught her injecting heroin into her toe. I told her to leave, then Dad came in and slapped me across the face. He's never hit me before. I'm not talking to him.

*Tuesday, November 12, 1997, 9:48 P.M.*

Lisa and Melissa had a huge fight today. They've both liked Kyle Janning since the beginning of the school year. Kyle asked Melissa to hang out after school.

When Lisa found out, she got super mad at Melissa for not inviting her. I don't really get why Lisa is angry. She should be jealous, but I don't think Melissa did anything wrong. That's what I said to Lisa, and now she's not talking to either of us.

*Friday, November 15, 1997, 10:35 P.M.*

Lisa apologized this morning and asked me to go to the

school play with her tonight. Crystal and Kelly went with us. It was lots of fun until we spotted Melissa with Kyle.

Lisa got quiet and wanted to go home as soon as the play was over. I went to Jack in the Box with Crystal and Kelly—we sat in our usual booth. It was packed after the play with lots of classmates. I'm lucky I'm part of a group, because some of the other poor kids at our school don't have any friends. If I wasn't working and making money to buy decent clothes, I'd be just like them.

***

Nick and Story walked hand in hand down Waikiki Beach, amidst throngs of tourists soaking in the morning sun. They did this every Saturday morning before eating breakfast at Eggs 'n Things and then settled in for a long day of studying at a campus library.

They were taking things slow at Story's request.

Nick didn't mind. He seemed to appreciate the time they had together, which was minimal because of his part-time baggage handler job at Hawaiian Airlines. He never complained.

When she asked him why he didn't, he said, "Complaining wastes time and energy."

Ever since Story announced that she was planning to apply to law school, her parents strongly recommended that she stop working. They even gave her extra spending money. She agreed.

When Nick was working, she was studying, and when they spent time together, it was usually at the library. It felt good to have an easygoing companion. On occasion, they'd watch a movie at her apartment while they held hands. They'd kiss. Then, he would return to his parents' condo in Makiki.

One night while studying at a campus center table, Nick asked her what she was planning to do for Thanksgiving.

"I always fly back to California to spend time with my family. What about you?"

"Restaurants are busy, so my parents work all weekend. I study and eat noodles." He smiled. "It's all right, I'm used to it."

"Would you like to come to California with me?" she asked, without thinking it through first.

He paused for a moment. "Sure, why not? I can try to fly on standby."

"No, I'll buy you a ticket. My gift to you." She had been saving money from her various jobs for several years. Mom and Kimberly had been quizzing her about Nick for weeks. Now, they'd get to meet him.

***

*Sunday, November 17, 1997, 4:20 P.M.*

Lolly's been hanging out here all day. Her voice is so shrill and she smells like mildew—she never bathes.

I've been holed up in my room, except for when I use the bathroom or get something to eat. I need Sundays to catch up on homework anyway. I spent all morning studying my chemistry book, which I find impossible to comprehend. I know I could ask Kyle Janning, the A+ science nerd, to tutor me. Wouldn't that piss off Lisa and Melissa? I would never do it, but it's funny to think about. Back to chemistry. Yuck!

*Monday, December 16, 1997, 8:17 P.M.*

The past month has been unbearable. I don't remember crying so much in my entire life. Where do I begin? Lolly read my journal and told Dad that I'm saving money to get away from him. He was furious and demanded I turn over the money. He said he'd go to the bank and tell them that he's my guardian and the account is illegal. Luckily, he doesn't know which bank, because I keep all the information in my purse.

*Thursday, December 19, 1997, 9:25 P.M.*

Dad is desperate to get his hands on my money. When I

came home yesterday, he was in my room and had thrown all my clothes on the bed. My food box is gone. He took my little pink jewelry box with the earrings Felicia gave me and the heart necklace I bought from a thrift shop. My jar of loose change was spilled all over the floor. Dad must have picked out all the quarters and dimes, because all that was left were pennies and a few nickels.

*Saturday, December 21, 1997, 7:20 P.M.*

Lolly was waiting for me when I got home. When I wasn't expecting it, she grabbed my arm and put her hands around my throat. She tried to choke me.

I used a technique I learned in P.E. during a self-defense class and was able to get free. Dad wasn't home. She kept yelling that I was wrecking her life and that I had stolen her money. She followed me into my room and wouldn't leave.

I finally convinced her that I'd hidden a twenty-dollar bill under the couch. When she left, I used a chair to barricade the door shut. I had to pee in a glass, because I'm afraid to leave my room.

Story closed the diary, then her eyes. She couldn't imagine ever being faced with someone choking her. If Zana had managed to get perfect grades under the worst of circumstances, there was no reason Story couldn't do anything she set her mind to do. Her finals had been horrific.

She wished she'd remembered to channel Zana during those late nights when she'd complained to Nick about having to spend all of her time studying. Now that she had been reminded of the girl's trials, she realized that her life was easy by comparison.

Story had flown home to California the night of her last final. Nick planned to fly standby on Christmas day when flights were fairly light. He was working double shifts until then to earn extra money, would spend Christmas Eve and morning with his parents, and the remaining weeks of school vacation with the Sanchez family. Thanksgiving had gone well, and Story's family had welcomed him with open arms.

On the way to the movie theater now, Kimberly asked Story, "Have you done it yet with Nick?"

Story gave her a quizzical look. "What?"

"Gone all the way?"

Story shook her head. Even if she had, she wasn't sure she'd tell her little sister, who was now a college student. Kimberly had pledged to a sorority and her life was far more exciting, with parties and plenty of fraternity boys to date. There was no way she would understand why Story had to be absolutely sure of a boy's true intensions before things got physical. Besides, she had a reputation as a good girl at UH and didn't want to destroy that with one mistake like she had in high school.

"Why do you ask?"

"Just wondering." Kimberly smiled slyly.

"What about you?" Story asked.

"I'm dating some guys." Kimberly laughed.

Story pulled Mom's Honda Accord into an open parking place at the movie theater parking lot. She turned to her sister and said, "Don't let any boy do anything you're not ready to do."

Kimberly looked puzzled.

"You have the power, Kimberly. Don't give it away to a boy. Once you do, he'll have all the power." As she said this, Story realized that she'd been trying to maintain power over Nick, which she no longer needed to do. She had grown to trust him. They were equals.

"Okay, sure."

"Just wait until you trust and love him first, okay?" Story pulled the keys out of the ignition and they headed to the theater to watch *Christmas with the Kranks.*

***

*Thursday, December 26, 1997, 6:05 P.M.*

On Christmas Eve Day, Dad and Lolly finally left the house. I didn't want to bother any of my friends during the holidays, so I used a luggage cart to haul my boxes and suitcase to a storage unit I had scoped out a few weeks ago, just in case I needed it. The place had sliding garage doors and twenty-four-hour access. There's even a public bathroom.

I told the man I'm eighteen years old and the unit is for my mother and I. He let me pay in cash.

After I rented the unit, I went to Goodwill and bought a fold up camping cot and a lantern. I've slept in the storage unit for two nights now. I think there are other people sleeping in their units, too. I hear the toilet flushing at night and I've seen a few people who don't look like they're moving stuff in and out.

*Friday, December 27, 1997, 7:15 P.M.*

I joined a YWCA down the street, so I have a place to shower. The last time I bathed was on Monday and I didn't want to wait any longer.

I worked yesterday and today and hoped no one thought I smelled. Tomorrow, I'm going to a laundromat. I'm sick of washing clothes out in the sink at the storage unit. The manager looked at me strangely when he saw me carrying a small pile of wet clothes. He didn't say anything, though.

*Sunday, December 29, 1997, 7:00 P.M.*

I've been so busy trying to escape from Dad that I haven't thought much about missing Christmas. Today, I worked out at the YWCA rather than sitting in my storage room and attracting attention.

I then wandered around a shopping mall and read in the library until it closed. I went to McDonald's for dinner. Now that I'm back in my storage unit, I'm lonely. I want to see my friends, but I'm embarrassed they might find out where I'm living.

*Wednesday, February 19, 1998, 11:45 P.M.*

The past few months have been crazy. The storage facility was bought by another company, which reduced their hours. The new owners locked the bathrooms after hours and installed security cameras. Big signs were posted warning that anyone on the premises after closing would be prosecuted.

I stayed at a homeless camp in a park for about a week, but I didn't sleep the entire time for fear I'd be attacked.

Lisa asked what was going on when I kept nodding off in class.

I lied and said I can't sleep, because Dad and Lolly are fighting. With her parents' permission, I'm now staying in their guest room with its own bathroom and a separate entrance. It's so nice to shower in a real shower again.

*Tuesday, March 25, 1998, 5:40 P.M.*

Last week, Lisa's parents told me I'd have to go back home, because they were getting ready to leave to go on vacation to Hawaii for spring break. I told them it's fine and pretended to go home.

They forgot to ask for their key, so after they left, I used it to get inside and sleep in the guest room. I'm keeping the lights off and am not going into any other rooms in the house.

# Chapter Twenty-four

Story was all smiles when she got her History of China midterm back. A four-point. Again. Her cumulative grade point average was 3.92. If she kept it up and scored well on the LSAT, she might get one of the coveted spots at UH's law school. If not, she'd probably go back to California.

Later, while studying with Nick, he seemed unusually quiet. He hadn't flashed his radiant smile all night. She assumed he'd gotten a bad grade on a test and didn't want to talk about it. On the way to her car, she asked him if everything was okay.

"You tell me." He glared at her.

"What's going on?" Story furrowed her brow.

He frowned and turned away from her. They walked down the parking garage steps in silence.

She touched his arm and asked, "Do we need to talk about something, Nick?"

He stopped and faced her. His eyes were brimming with tears. "We've been going out for eight months and it seems like you don't even like me."

"What do you mean?"

Tears fell down Nick's face. He grabbed her hand. "I love you, Story."

Her heart swelled at his words. She hadn't wanted to be the first one to say it.

"I love you, too, honey." She let herself be swept up in his arms, and for the first time, she gave in to his deep kisses, feeling no need to put on the brakes.

***

*Thursday, April 10, 1998, 9:15 P.M.*

Just before Lisa's family came back from Hawaii, I found a room for rent in the basement of an old lady's house. Mrs. Diaz charges $50 per week and I have to do some cleaning and yard work.

She said she wanted to rent to a man, but I insisted that I could do the work. She thinks I'm twenty-one years old. She wears really thick glasses.

*Monday, May 5, 1998, 8:25 P.M.*

I've been living on my own for over four months. It seems like four years. My life isn't that much different than it was when I was with Dad, except I don't have to be as careful about hiding my money. I still keep a box of food in the closet of the room I'm renting. I'm still careful about where I put what I call my valuables, because I don't know if Mrs. Diaz comes into my room when I'm at school or work.

Now that I have to do chores at home in order to keep this place, I don't have any time left over to hang out with my friends. Lisa, Kelly, and Melissa all have boyfriends now and don't have much time for me anyway.

*Thursday, May 8, 1998, 10:55 P.M.*

My heart is racing. I can't sleep. Mrs. Diaz said that my father stopped by the house today. He told her that I'm only fifteen years old and have to come home.

I told her that he has a mental illness and still thinks of me as a child.

She looked like she didn't believe me.

I offered to cook dinner. After I made stir fried chicken and vegetables with what I found in her fridge and then washed dishes and cleaned up everything, she said I acted a lot older than my twenty-one years.

*Monday, May 12, 1998, 7:30 P.M.*

I told Felicia everything today. She called me into her office and asked why I've been late to work at least once each week this year. I spilled the beans about escaping from Dad and Lolly.

She then told me the real reason for her concern. Dad had come by and threatened to call CPS.

I broke down and cried in front of her. I'm sick of this, but I can't go back. Felicia said she had an idea. She had to go to a meeting, but said she'll have time to talk about it later in the week. She told me to hang in there a little while longer.

*Friday, May 16, 1998, 8:45 P.M.*

There was a note on my door when I got home. Mrs. Diaz wants to talk with me. This can't be good.

*Saturday, May 17, 1998, 9:35 P.M.*

Mrs. Diaz said she knows I'm lying about my age. She gave me until Tuesday to move out. I don't know where to go. Lisa's family has made it clear they need to reserve their guest room for real guests.

I might be able to stay overnight at Melissa's or Kelly's houses, but not for more than a day or two.

There are a few ads with rooms for rent, but they're with men. One of the guys said he'd prefer to rent to a single woman. I wonder if he wants an underage girl? No thanks! I'm sick of this.

*Tuesday, May 20, 1998, 8:20 P.M.*

I spent the day moving everything I had at Mrs. Diaz's house into my storage unit, except for a suitcase of clothes and toiletries. By 5:00 P.M., I hadn't found a place to live, so I'm staying at a homeless shelter.

I've got the top bunk. A large woman with horrible bumps all over her face is sleeping below me. I didn't want to eat their food, so I went to McDonald's for dinner.

I tried to rent a hotel room at a few places, but I don't think they wanted to rent to a teenager. One lady told me this, and another said there was a waiting list for the room. I know she was lying.

***

On their first day of summer vacation, Nick came by Story's apartment and surprised her with a bouquet of tropical flowers.

"What's this?" she asked, taking it.

"Beautiful flowers for a beautiful girl." Nick pulled her in for a long kiss. "Now, come on. I packed a picnic lunch."

"Where are we going?" Story's eyes widened. He'd never taken her on a picnic before and seldom surprised her with flowers. He liked to talk over their plans in advance.

"You'll see," he assured her.

"Am I dressed okay?" She'd put on a light sundress and Nick was wearing a dress shirt with shorts—an odd combination.

He winked at her. "Perfect."

They hopped into his Kia and he drove towards Makiki.

"Are we going to your place?" she asked.

He smiled but didn't say anything.

As they approached his condo building, she wondered if they were having lunch with his parents. He then drove past it and up towards the mountains.

When he started driving up the switchbacks, she guessed they were going to the museum, but they passed it and continued up to the very top, where he parked at Round Top.

He helped her out of the car and grabbed the picnic basket. But, before they walked to the grassy area, he pulled off his dress shirt. Underneath, he wore a tuxedo t-shirt.

She laughed. His goofy sense of humor often delighted her.

They set up their picnic in the grassy area with a stunning view of Diamond Head, Waikiki, and downtown Honolulu. They could see as far as Pearl Harbor. It was a sunny day with few clouds.

He unpacked the bento lunches, and as they ate, he sat close to her and laughed at her story about one of her favorite professors.

"Would you like dessert?" He leaned over and kissed her.

"Was that my dessert?" She laughed and pulled him in closer.

"I've got your favorite."

Story wasn't sure what that would be, because all desserts were her favorite.

He pulled out a big bakery box and opened it. There were pieces of chocolate, carrot, and lemon cake, slices of cherry and banana crème pies, several donuts, and a half dozen assorted cookies.

Story put her hand to her mouth. "You're not kidding!"

"Story, you're the sweetest woman I've ever met. I want our lives together to be like a never-ending dessert." He got on one knee, pulled a small box from his pocket, and grabbed her hand. "With you, my life is a story and will have a happy ending."

He opened the little box to reveal a diamond engagement ring. "Stephanie Sanchez, will you do me the honor of becoming my wife? Will you marry me?"

Her eyes lit up and her smile broadened with each word. "Yes! Yes!"

He placed the ring on her finger, and she melted into his arms.

***

*Tuesday, June 10, 1998, 8:10 P.M.*

Happy birthday to me! The one thing both of my parents had in common was they didn't celebrate birthdays. Mom and Dad met in a small community in which everyone went to the same church that didn't allow the celebration of birthdays.

When they were sixteen years old, Mom got pregnant with me. Their parents told them they were a disgrace and had to leave. That's how they ended up moving to California, and that's why I've never met any of my relatives.

Now that I'm sixteen years old and on my own, I'm celebrating my birthday. I bought a big chocolate cupcake with sprinkles. I didn't have a candle, but I made a wish anyway. My wish came true! Later today, I took my driver's test and passed. Yay me!

*Friday, June 14, 1998, 8:20 P.M.*

Felicia doesn't know I'm living in this shelter. I'd be too embarrassed to tell her. I'm looking for another room to rent, but no one wants to rent to a sixteen-year-old. If I buy a car, I'll be able to live in it.

I've saved over $1,000, but I'm not sure I can find a car that works, and I'm worried that I won't have money for food and gas if I use all my savings. I told the shelter organizers that I'm eighteen years old. If they found out I'm a minor, they'd call CPS.

I think they believe I'm an adult, because I have a job at law firm. On the other hand, I'm not sure they can figure out why I'm homeless. I earn money, but no one will rent me a place, because I don't have an ID showing I'm an adult.

*Monday, June 17, 1998, 8:00 P.M.*

Felicia filed a lawsuit for me today. She's asking the court that I become an emancipated minor. She explained that it was not in my best interest for my dad to exert any control over my life, and that the foster system had failed me.

If the court grants the petition, I'll be able to sign contracts without my dad's permission. I'll be able to rent a room, go to college, and get medical care. Felicia said she expects that my dad will object.

I had to sign an affidavit saying that I'm working and supporting myself and my dad is a drug addict. I also had to say that I was raped while in a foster home, so that's not an option for me.

I'm going to be a senior in high school in August and only have a few classes to take before I get my diploma in December. If I'm emancipated, I can take college classes while finishing up high school.

*Friday, June 21, 1998, 7:40 P.M.*

In order to stay at this shelter, I had to agree to a counseling session with the shelter's psychologist. I explained that I left my dad's house due to his drug use.

The counselor—I forgot her name already—said that I have to address my feelings from Dad's abandonment.

I always thought I had abandoned him by leaving, but she said that his choice to use drugs rather than take care of his daughter is on him. He's the one who left me.

Wow! I've been feeling guilty for not taking care of him, leaving, and filing the lawsuit (of course, I didn't tell the counselor that I'm not eighteen). I feel like a weight has been lifted off my shoulders.

*Sunday, June 23, 1998, 8:10 P.M.*

I bought a used Buick Riviera today! My first car! It has some body damage on the passenger side, but it runs. The best thing is that it has a trunk for my stuff and a backseat I can sleep on.

Tim, the guy who sold it to me, had been trying to sell it for months with no offers. He just wanted to get it off his hands. He has three other cars and no place to park the Riviera. He kept getting parking tickets if he forgot to move it in time. He wanted $1,200 for it, but I said I only had $500, so he took it. He said he would have to sell it to a junkyard otherwise.

Tomorrow, I plan to move out of here.

*Friday, August 15, 1998, 8:50 P.M.*

The summer is almost over and all I've done is work and survive. It takes a lot of time to find a place to park my car overnight where I can safely sleep. I can't park it in the same place, or someone might figure out what I'm doing. I have to park it in a dark place so no one sees into the backseat, and if it's too bright, I can't sleep.

On the other hand, it's scary in dark places. I worry that someone might try to break into my car with me in it. One night, that almost happened, and I screamed so loud I scared the guy away.

I have to get up two hours before work in order to drive to the Y to shower. I usually have a short workout first. Breakfast is a McDonald's Egg McMuffin and orange juice.

I wish I had a refrigerator. I miss being able to have a bowl of cereal with milk or a cold drink. I can't save any food that has to be refrigerated. It takes a lot of time and money to go to a store or restaurant for every meal.

On weekends, I spend hours at a laundromat and then have to carefully fold my clothes and put them in my trunk. I don't have an iron and can't hang my clothes. I put all the extra stuff in my storage unit and have to pop by there to get things I need every now and then. When school starts, I'll be working, taking classes, and studying, and this will be a lot more difficult.

*Tuesday, September 9, 1998, 7:50 P.M.*

I don't know how I'm going to sleep tonight. My court hearing is tomorrow. Felicia said the judge will ask questions about how I'm going to take care of myself if emancipation is awarded.

I finally told her that I've been living in my car.

Her eyes welled up with tears. She thought I was renting a room in a house.

I assured her that I've saved up enough money to rent a room once I'm legally able to.

She patted my shoulder and said, "Let's do this."

## Chapter Twenty-five

It had been three weeks since Story and Nick had taken the LSAT. After Story's morning classes, she stopped by the computer lab to check her email. Nick must have had the same idea and was already there and logging on.

"Remember, we look at them together." Story logged onto her email at the computer next to her fiancé's. "Did you get the results email?"

Nick nodded. "Did you?"

"Yeah." Story felt her throat constrict. She was anxious to know her score, but if she hadn't done well, she wasn't sure how she'd handle the disappointment. "Let's look at the same time." She swallowed hard.

"Okay." Nick paused. "Open your email on one." They each positioned their finger on their mouse. "Okay, three, two, one." They both clicked their emails open.

"What did you get?" Story tried to assess Nick's expression.

"I…ah, 162 out of 180." He smiled. "And you?"

"Congratulations!" She tried to be happy for him. "I only got a 156."

"Very good, sweetheart. You should be very proud of yourself."

"Will that be high enough to get into UH?" She furrowed her brow. She didn't think so.

"It should be no problem at all with your high grades." He clicked off the computer and turned to her. "I don't think we need to worry at all."

Story raised her eyebrows. She would worry until she got an acceptance letter.

They walked hand in hand to their next class. The first hurdle was over. Next, the admissions process. If they both got into UH, they'd have a June wedding on Oahu. If not—well, Story didn't want to think about it.

***

*Wednesday, September 10, 1998, 8:15 P.M.*

I saw Dad for the first time since I left in December. He looks like he's seventy years old. His skin is yellowish, he's painfully skinny, he's hunched over, and he shuffles when he walks.

He came up to me and gave me a hug and kissed my cheek. He smelled like old socks. I guess I still love him, but I'm still angry. How could he dishonor Mom by treating me like this?

When he talked to the judge, his hands shook and his voice was raspy. His promise to give me a good home did not match his appearance. The judge asked if he worked and Dad said no, but he could get a job.

There was nothing about him that would convince anyone that he was capable of working or that he had a shot at being hired. I testified about what life was like with Dad and that I've had to take care of myself since I was very young. I even told them about the box of food I stashed in the closet, but that Dad and Lolly stole it.

Under oath, I admitted I was living in my Riviera, but if I'm emancipated, I can legally rent a room. The judge took a recess for lunch, heard some more testimony, and then took the case under advisement.

Felicia doesn't know how long it will take to get a decision. She said we might lose and then I'd either have to go back to Dad or to a foster home. No way!

*Friday, September 12, 1998, 2:35 A.M.*

I'm so scared. A few hours ago, I was sleeping in the backseat of my car, but was woken up by pounding on the windows. I quickly crawled over the middle part of the front seat and started the car with the key I keep in the center console for just this type of situation (it's happened once before).

I drove to an all-night launderette. I'm parked under a streetlamp while writing this. No more sleep tonight.

I'm desperate for this situation to change. I can't take it anymore.

*Monday, September 15, 1998, 6:30 P.M.*

The moment I walked into the law office this morning Felicia rushed up to me. She led me to her office, closed the door, and yelped, "We won! You're an emancipated minor." We jumped up and down in unison. I couldn't believe it. The court system saved me.

*Tuesday, September 16, 1998, 7:15 A.M.*

I barely slept last night. My heart was pounding out of my chest with excitement for the future. I can't wait to finally take control of my life. For the first time, I dared to think beyond my next meal. During a break in the court proceedings last week, Felicia asked me if I ever thought about going to law school. I laughed it off. How could a foster kid ever afford college, do well enough to get accepted into a law school, and then actually pay for it? It would be amazing to be a lawyer, but I need to be realistic. Maybe, I can go to community college and study to be a paralegal.

*Friday, September 19, 1998, 8:30 P.M.*

I was able to rent a furnished room in a nice house in a decent neighborhood. I can shower in the en suite bathroom. There's a mini fridge and microwave in my room, and I have access to the main kitchen as well. I put the food from my reserve food stash in the cupboards and threw away the box. I'm done with hoarding food or anything else.

My favorite part of my room is the closet. I neatly hung up my clothes and put the rest in dresser drawers. Felicia is helping me with the paperwork and everything I need to comply with the court order. I know I'm going to make it work.

*Wednesday, September 24, 1998, 7:15 P.M.*

Felicia called me into her office today. She wanted to know what my plans are now that I'm an emancipated minor.

I sat back in a chair facing her for a few minutes, letting the feeling of control over my own destiny wash over me.

I told her that I found the perfect room with a lock on the door and from there, I'd make everything up as I went along. I didn't say anything of my hope to someday attend community college and become a paralegal. She caught me looking at her law school diploma on the wall, and again said that she thought I'd be a good lawyer. I shrugged and changed the subject. It's all too much to think about right now.

I'm laying on my bed. The room smells clean. My stomach isn't rumbling. The door is locked, and I know I'll get a good night's sleep.

Now that my life is so much better, Dear Diary, I'm sorry, but you're no longer going to live with me. You belong hidden in my car trunk with all of my sad memories. I'm starting a new chapter (and diary) today!

***

Story closed Zana's diary and sighed. She'd read the pages so often over the years that the bindings had broken and large rubber bands now held them together. Sometimes, she wondered what her life would have been like if Zana hadn't taught her about gratitude. When Story thought back to that day when she had opened the trunk of the old Buick and her feelings of disappointment over her parents not buying her a new car, her face reddened in shame.

Her thoughts were interrupted by a text. It was from Nick, asking her what she was doing.

She paused and wrote back. Visiting an old, dear friend.

# #Epilogue

*2017*

The early morning was the busiest. Story packed lunches for their six- and eight-year-old daughters, and then Nick drove them to Punahou on his way to work. He worked at the real estate transaction section of the law firm where Story had interned many years ago—Gravelle, Parsons & Dell. After they left, she spent a half hour tidying up the place and then headed to her office in Kapolei, which was conveniently located near family court.

Today, Story was meeting a client in the morning and then would head to town for the Women Lawyer's Forum at the YWCA at lunch. She'd never been to the event before, but Nick had bought her the ticket and urged her to attend. As a busy working mother, he felt that she needed to make some female friends.

She hadn't argued.

As she drove to the luncheon, it occurred to her that she had no idea what the program would be. She'd forgotten to look at the flyer and didn't have time to do a Google search to find out.

She took a seat at a table with a half-dozen other women lawyers, then walked through the buffet lunch as they talked about their law practices. The other women worked in middle to large-sized firms—mostly practicing litigation. When the program was about to begin, the room hushed and three young women took their places in the front, each wired with a lapel microphone.

The moment she heard the first woman's name, Story became mesmerized. It was Zana West—the girl whose diary she'd read all those years ago. And, to her surprise, she was a new associate at her husband's law firm in the litigation division on the floor below his. Nick didn't work with the litigation attorneys and only knew a few of them. She'd be surprised if he'd ever met Zana.

Zana talked about the struggles she'd had as an undergraduate and law student. She'd had to work, apply for grants, loans, and scholarships in order to pay for tuition and room and board. Zana said that she hadn't thought that a foster kid could ever become a lawyer and so at one point, she planned on being a paralegal. Her teachers and a mentor encouraged her to set her sights higher. She shared a little about her homelessness, then talked about how these experiences had shaped her legal career. She had gone into litigation because she'd wanted to have a secure job and make a comfortable living in order to avoid homelessness in her future.

Story couldn't keep her eyes off of Zana. When the program ended, she made a beeline for her.

"Zana, my name is Story Lin. I'm a homeless rights advocate and family lawyer in Kopolei." She reached out and shook Zana's hand.

"Hi Story, nice to meet you."

"I'm originally from Ventura."

Zana's eyes widened. "My hometown."

"In 2000, my parents bought me a used car—a Buick Riviera." Story paused as she watched Zana's face carefully to see how she'd react. "I'm quite certain it had been yours."

Zana's mouth opened and then closed as her mind registered the news. She said nothing.

"I found your diaries in the trunk of the car."

"Oh, my God." Zana put her hand to her mouth. "Did you read them?"

Story nodded. "Don't worry. It's not what you think. I was a spoiled country club kid. Your diaries changed my life."

"How?" Zana's shoulders relaxed.

"I learned that there were other people in the world that didn't have things as good as my parents and I. Reading about your experiences made me appreciate all of my blessings. You were an excellent student, which motivated me to study hard, get good grades, and ultimately go to law school. I had no idea you'd gone to law school, too—and moved to Hawaii."

"Are you serious?" Zana's eyebrows shot up. "I had no idea that I had motivated anyone. I was just a messed up kid. As you can see, I'm no longer that beanpole, wisp of a teenager."

They both laughed in unison.

Story could see that Zana was now wearing what looked like an expensive suit with matching pumps and her posture was that of a confident attorney, rather than the girl of so long ago.

"I was even more messed up before I read your diaries," Story said. "I don't know what would have happened to me if I hadn't learned all the lessons you taught me through your challenges." Story started to tear up and Zana gave her a hug. "My husband and I even competed in a triathlon because of you."

Zana laughed. "I'm so happy we finally met. I appreciate you so much for sharing this with me."

"Do you mind if I ask you a question?" Story hesitated.

"Sure."

"How's your father?"

Zana grimaced. "We didn't have contact for years. Before I graduated from law school, he wrote me a letter. He claims that he's changed and he begged to see me. I asked him to mail me a check stub from his employer first. I haven't received anything, and that's the last I've heard from him."

"I'm sorry." Story looked down at her feet. She hoped that she hadn't ruined their encounter.

"It's okay." Zana smiled and put her hand on Story's shoulder.

"It's hard for me to even describe to you how much your story meant to me." Story choked up again, paused, and then reached for her phone in her purse. She pulled up a picture. "These are my two daughters. The oldest is named Zana and the youngest is Felicia."

Story watched as Zana raised her eyebrows.

Story placed a hand on Zana's arm. "I have one more question for you. How did you manage to be so strong?"

Zana paused and thought for a few moments. "Hope. I could only hope for a better future. When everything fell apart, I always had hope."

Story nodded and smiled. "How can I get your diaries back to you?"

Zana smiled. "That's not my life anymore. You can keep them."

Story thought a moment. When her daughters were old enough, she planned to let them read about their namesakes, and only hoped they would be as inspired as she was.

@ZLaw

Who would have imagined that the diaries of a poor, messed up girl would make any difference for anyone? I'm stunned. After I met Story, I searched for my dad on Instagram, and there he was. He looks healthy and was even posing on a triathlon bike. Miracles happen!

## ***Want to read more about Zana West and her adventures? Check out the Tri-Angles Series and learn about Zana's life in Honolulu, Hawaii.***

**BOOK 1**

***Land Sharks:***

***#HonoluluLaw, #Triathletes & a #TVStar***

Young attorney, Zana West, is assigned the perfect case for a triathlete—a lawsuit filed by Brad Jordan, a man who claims he was paralyzed during the Honolulu Olympic triathlon trials. As an added bonus, Zana's television crush, Jerry Hirano, the star of "Fighting in Paradise" by night and attorney-by-day playboy, represents another defendant in the case. ***Land Sharks*** takes readers on a swim through the murky waters of Honolulu law, a spin through the competitive world of triathlon, and a sprint through the set of a Hawaii TV show.

**BOOK 2**

***Freewheel:***

***#HonoluluLaw, #FamousTriathlete, & a #Charity***

Young and ambitious new attorney Zana West is hired to represent Ryan Peterson and provide him a defense in a lawsuit, but by doing so, her relationship with Jerry Hirano, T.V. star of "Fighting in Paradise," is threatened. Will Zana be able to help Ryan get his life back and keep her relationship together? ***Freewheel*** takes readers for a spin in the real world of personal injury litigation, where the drama takes place outside the courtroom.

**BOOK 3**

**VO2 Max:**

**#HonoluluLaw, #Protriathletes, & a #Sports Agent**

In VO2 Max, attorneys Zana West's and Jerry Hirano's relationship is at risk when new challenges develop as Zana takes on a new career track as a sports agent. Will their love survive all the changes? And can Zana help new pro-triathletes, Haley O'Neill and Sean Bennett, stay on the right path? ***VO2 Max*** takes readers for a spin in the fast and newly glamorous world of professional triathlon.

# Acknowledgements

Although I wrote this book well before the Covid-19 pandemic, it was published after the world spent more than a year in various stages of lockdown. My personal world grew smaller as I spent most of my time at home, at my office, and in the drive thru line at Starbucks. Zoom expanded my reach during the pandemic, allowing me to make many new friends even though we've never had the opportunity to shake hands or hug.

A special thank you to all of you who have brought joy into my life during a challenging time when sometimes the only people I saw in person were the friendly faces at Starbucks and Safeway. Mahalo to those special baristas who wrote encouraging notes on my egg bite wrappers. I could truly see the smiles behind your masks.

Much love and thank you to my boyfriend, Bill Touth. Although we can't be in the same state or even visit each other due to the pandemic, his frequent phone calls and texts provide love and support.

Hugs to my Zumba family whom I danced with for hours each week, mostly on Zoom and Facebook Live. Some of you, I haven't even met in person, but I feel like we are good friends: Amy Kotani, Izzy Ibarra, RJ Raymundo, MJ Sarmiento, Suzanne Hiramoto, Millie and Vernon Tatsuno, Carlito Unzueta, Carolina de Calisto, and so many more.

When we re-opened, I was blessed to reunite with my Zumba sisters, Danni Bennett, Haylee Bennett, Nadine Frost, and Yashia Navarro. They are truly my tribe, and we shared so much during this special time. I dearly miss Susan Tyau and Lilinoe Yong, but we'll dance together soon. Mahalo to the lovely addition to our sisterhood—Branz Hikalea-Kanae.

The hope of going to the Tokyo Olympics together was extinguished, but a special shout-out to my close friends, Dianne Johannson and Christine Lynders. There will be many adventures to come, and even game nights sans masks with Brian Rosa and Barb Johannson.

Mahalo to my editor, Brittiany Koren, for her continued support. My fourth book in this series would not have happened without her. I wouldn't have published any fiction without the support of my writer's group—Steve Novak, Brian Malanaphy, and Karin O'Mahony.

Thank you to other dear friends Mark Coberly, Cindi John, Mary Alexander, Glenn Uesugi, Jennifer Papastephanou, Lisa and Jim Ghahremani, Angela Hayslett, Dr. Kristie Byrum, Cheri Huber, Colleen Graham, Ramona Emerson, Lesia Schafer, Kristina Selset, Tamara Gerrard, Elaine Gallant, Karin Polivy, Nathalie Pettit, Melissa Deats, Heather McVay, Marilyn Bontrager, June Hoffman, Deborah Blackman, Prebah and Ivan Covetz, Winston Dang, and so many others who support me and my work.

A special mahalo to ThinkTech Hawaii president Jay Fidel, who allows me to create my show, The Wide World of Esports each week. And, mahalo to my HAIP, IAIP, ESTA, and EBA friends and colleagues.

Thank you so very much to Celeste Moore and Lenore Ogawa for all that you have done to make my office a success.

And a special thank you to my supportive and loving family: Kim and Hannah Nohr, Gerrie Nohr, Jill, Gordy, and Drew Gradwohl, Jay Iversen, Jeff Iversen, Paul Wilson, Christian Wilson, Marsha Fu, Emily Fu, Elliot and Jenny Fu, Oli Fu, Melissa Fu, the Sheffield family, the Graves family, the Wilson family, and the Fu family. Love you all!

# About the Author

Katharine M. Nohr is the author of *Managing Risk in Sport and Recreation: The Essential Guide for Loss Prevention* (Human Kinetics, 2009) and the Tri-Angles series, which include *Land Sharks, Freewheel,* and *VO2 Max* (Written Dreams Publishing, 2016, 2017, 2018). She is the host of the weekly talk show, "The Wide World of Esports" on the ThinkTech Hawaii livestreaming network. She is an insurance defense and Esports attorney and a principal in Nohr Sports Risk Management, LLC.

During her free time, Katharine dances Zumba, swims, and plays with her Siamese cats, Ninja and Ramsey. Find her on social media at @KatharineNohr or @TriathlonNovels.

CPSIA information can be obtained
at www.ICGtesting.com
Printed in the USA
LVHW032339190721
693160LV00003B/374

9 781951 375218